I0597903

TRIAL OF THE STAR DRAGON

AN EARTH FORCE SKY PATROL FILE: SOLAR YEAR 2388

BLAZE WARD

KNOTTED ROAD PRESS

Trial of the Star Dragon
An Earth Force Sky Patrol File: Solar Year 2388
Blaze Ward
Copyright © 2019 Blaze Ward
All rights reserved
Published by Knotted Road Press
www.KnottedRoadPress.com

ISBN: 978-1-64470-059-4

Cover art:
ID 119989394 © 3000ad | DepositPhoto.com

Cover and interior design copyright © 2019 Knotted Road Press

Never miss a release!
If you'd like to be notified of new releases, sign up for my newsletter.

I will never spam you, or use your email for nefarious purposes. You can also unsubscribe at any time.

http://www.blazeward.com/newsletter/

This book is licensed for your personal enjoyment only. All rights reserved. This is a work of fiction. All characters and events portrayed in this book are fictional, and any resemblance to real people or incidents is purely coincidental. This book, or parts thereof, may not be reproduced in any form without permission.

ALSO BY BLAZE WARD

The Jessica Keller Chronicles

Auberon

Queen of the Pirates

Last of the Immortals

Goddess of War

Flight of the Blackbird

The Red Admiral

St. Legier

Winterhome

CS-405

Queen Anne's Revenge

Packmule

Persephone

Additional Alexandria Station Stories

The Story Road

Siren

Two Bottles of Wine with a War God

The Science Officer Series

The Science Officer

The Mind Field

The Gilded Cage

The Pleasure Dome

The Doomsday Vault

The Last Flagship

The Hammerfield Gambit

The Hammerfield Payoff

Earth Force Sky Patrol

Birth of the Star Dragon

Flight of the Star Dragon

Call of the Star Dragon

Shadow of the Star Dragon

Trial of the Star Dragon

Other Science Fiction Stories

Myrmidons

Moonshot

Menelaus

Earthquake Gun

Moscow Gold

Fairchild

White Crane

The Collective Universe

The Shipwrecked Mermaid

Imposters

AWAKENING

THE LIGHT WAS SO BRIGHT, so disorienting that it took him several seconds to remember something as trivial as his name.

Gareth St. John Dankworth.

Earth Force Sky Patrol

Accord of Souls Constabulary.

For several moments he wondered if he was dead. Stories he had heard when he was young had suggested that such a perfect, white light that surrounded you when Heaven called you to your final resting place.

He wasn't ready to be dead. There was still at least one man he needed to make sure preceded him, after all. Marc Sarzynski. Maximus. The worst criminal mastermind in the entire, known galaxy.

The man who had been his best friend for nearly a decade when they were younger.

But then other voices intruded on Gareth's consciousness. Ones he recognized.

Hopefully, they hadn't died, too. He would rather

be lonely in heaven, or hell, than to have all those others, those friends, join him.

But that was most certainly out of his hands now.

He looked up as a room seemed to come into being around him.

Around them.

White, but he was expecting that. Somehow larger than the sky, and yet it still felt tiny. Compact.

Overfull with emotions and beings.

And then Gareth understood who those beings were, the immense ones up on that platform, looking down at him and the other ghosts standing with him on the floor.

Was it a floor? There was something solid holding him up, but he could see stars through it and the walls, like they were all ghosts, too. And through the other ghosts in here with him. The air smelled like spring, right after that first good rain that makes all the plants wake up and look around. There was even a breeze that seemed to stir the air, so maybe he was onto something.

Jackeith Grodray. Eveth Baker. Those two were easy to recognize. Their intensity stood out against the others. Cops going to make perhaps the most important arrest of their already-storied careers.

Talyarkinash Liamssen. Doctor. Geneticist. Nari. Friend. The woman who would not allow the other two to leave her behind as he and the two of them walked into what might be their final battle.

Others were familiar, scattered through the space and indistinct, like they kept wanting to turn to smoke and never could quite make it.

Gareth opened his mouth and nothing came out.

Nothing? How was that possible?

No. Unacceptable.

"Who are you?" he managed to whisper.

The powerful being at the center of the dais above turned to face him, shock somehow registering on the face that appeared almost human. Almost Vanir.

Almost a god.

Gareth understood then, who they were.

All twelve of them had similar faces, similar features, that blend of Vanir and something else, but they looked almost like images projected on the side of a building, so huge they were compared to the folks down here on the ground with Gareth.

At the same time, they also appeared as tremendous clouds, white with energy and power.

Those were the Chaa themselves. The most powerful of the ancients. The ones who had shaped the *Accord of Souls* into a fixed form before transforming themselves into something else and setting out to find the Creator of the Universe, so they could sit at His knee and learn of His Plan.

"You would speak for the Humans?" the being communicated in a way that Gareth heard with his entire body, and not just his pointy, Vanir ears.

Speak for the Humans? Could he even do that? Gareth wasn't human anymore, at least as far as he knew.

Talyarkinash had transformed him physically into a Vanir, among other things, along with the help of the two Yuudixtl scientists/criminals: Morty and Xiomber.

Except he wasn't **OF** the *Accord of Souls*. Did not belong to that psionic collective that bound seventeen other species into the peace, the galaxy-spanning republic of worlds that excluded only the *Earth* from its halls.

"I am no longer Human," Gareth forced the words out with his mind, rather than his diaphragm. "But I would speak. For Justice, perhaps."

"It is noted, Gareth St. John Dankworth," the creature (Man? Being? Chaa?) said. "Who else would speak."

"If it is to be a judgment, then my words should be known," another voice spoke up.

Gareth did not hear it with his ears. Perhaps his soul?

But he knew that voice.

Royston Loughty, PhD, WMU, FRS, CBE, CStJ. Doctor of Physics. Warden of the Mathematical Union. Fellow of the Royal Society. Commander, British Empire. Commander, Order of St John.

More importantly, the Father of Philippa Loughty, the woman Gareth had been on his way to finally propose to when all this craziness began a year ago. *Pippa.*

How was Dr. Loughty here? Who else had joined him? Them?

"But for my arrogance, we would not be here," Dr. Loughty pronounced. "If a price must be paid, perhaps my soul will be of sufficient weight to offset the innocent."

"There are no innocents here," the Chaa in charge spoke. "Only shades of guilt beginning with troublesome and ending in xenocide. Who would speak for the *Accord of Souls*?"

A pause stretched, before another illuminated ghost stepped forward. He glowed white, like the rest, but Gareth got the impression of blueness from the man.

"In the absence of the Proctor, I suppose that such responsibility falls on my shoulders, Lord," the person said. "I would have led the *Accord* into making such a terrible decision, had you not intervened."

"The decision yet remains outstanding, Petim Diazal," the Chaa responded. "*The Communion* is gathered in Congress to judge."

Gareth heard most of the room now, erupting into whispers of awe and fear.

The Communion? The *Twelve* most powerful of the Chaa? The ones who had created everything? Here? Now?

Gathered In Judgment did not sound hopeful.

"How shall I address you, Lord?" the man known as Petim Diazal asked in a penitent voice.

"I am *Speaker For The Communion*," the Chaa pronounced. "The *Twelve* are gathered. All of the *Ascended Chaa* listen in on this deliberation, that they may make their wills known ere Judgment is rendered."

Gareth had studied some aspects of *Accord* history and law, in his quest to earn himself a proper place in the Constabulary, the police forces that protected the *Accord*.

A race of powerful mentalists known as The Chaa had found the way to free themselves from physical bodies. With immortality assured, they had set out to find the Creator, but before they left, fifty thousand years ago, they had taken most of the Chaa, those who did not wish to live forever, and transformed them into the Vanir.

Those Left Behind.

At the same time, they had chosen sixteen other species from across the galaxy and *Uplifted* them to sentience and civilization, where most had been barely animals at the time. Nari. Warreth. Yuudixtl. Grace. Quarrie. Elohynn. Borren. Moisa. Th'Tarni. Vratha. Enjev. Arawath. Ramasayia. Traakna. Drahvi. U'Chagi.

The *Accord of Souls.*

The *Twelve*, according to legend, had stood on the surface of their homeworld, *Almar*, the *Axle of Time*, and leapt into eternity. That hallowed soil today held the government buildings of the *Accord* itself, although Gareth had only ever seen pictures of it.

Gareth watched as one by one, the twelve beings before him lit up in turn and communicated their sigil to the assembly. It wasn't a name. Wasn't just a name. Instead, it somehow conveyed their entire being, their purpose.

First Immortal.

Docent, also known as the *Great Teacher.*

Seeker for the Knee of God.

Uplifter.

Glory in Sunrise.

Merciless, conveying implacable power as well as great sadness.

Speaker For The Communion.

Narrator of History.

Mountain.

Astray in Darkness.

Magistrate.

Last Traveler.

Of all of them, *Last Traveler* seemed to be the

friendliest. Gareth caught a hint of true warmth as the being spoke.

"We are gathered in judgment," *Speaker For The Communion* pronounced. "Explanations will be heard. Guilt will be weighed. Worlds will be altered. The *Accord* must be protected."

Gareth felt his breath catch at that last bit.

"Why?" he demanded.

It sounded weak, even to his own ears, but he would not, could not remain silent.

"Who challenges?" *Speaker For The Communion*'s voice seemed to roar.

"Gareth Dankworth," he replied. "If you are truly gods, you Chaa, you could fix everything. Your failures of vision have brought us thus."

Inwardly, he gasped at his own audacity.

Certainly, Gareth expected that he should wash his own mouth out with soap for speaking to a god that way, but he could not stay his own rage at the situation. From the stirrings on the platform, Gareth expected someone to strike him down with lightning now.

Or at least snap him on the wrist with a ruler, like the sisters had once done when a pupil spoke out of turn.

Last Traveler brightened, drawing all eyes his(?) direction.

"The Human speaks truth," *Last Traveler* pronounced in a sharp, doom-calling tone. "We chose to exclude his type from the *Accord* during the organizing vote. That they did not subsequently chose to follow our Great Plan for their civilizing development is not necessarily a crime we should place at their feet. There are others much more culpable whom we should address first."

Gareth watched the creatures on the platform make their wishes known with light and sound. It would be easier if they had corporeal form, but each still seemed to manifest as a glowing cloud of gray/white light that was at times painful to even look at, rather than a body, and even the faces came and went as he watched.

But Gareth knew they had once shared a form similar to his own, even as he would have still looked somewhat like a human if he had a proper form.

Seven feet, four inches tall. Three hundred and forty pounds in his fighting trim. He could still pass a large human, such as the monsters of the interior, defensive line, even though he had played defensive end in school.

That much, Vanir were just large humans, externally. The ears were dramatically oversized and came to points, much like the elves that many fantasy artists liked to create. His eyes were larger, relative to the rest of his skull as well, almost like a cartoon character.

But he was also among the biggest, strongest of the Vanir he had met. Morty and Xiomber had done that on purpose, because they had transformed Marc Sarzynski the exact same way. The same build. Everything. Only the coloration was different, with Marc's normally darker skin and dark, curly hair preserved, even as Gareth's blond hair had.

They had at least started there. Before they moved on at Gareth's insistence and did something for which these gods in attendance might truly take offence. They had turned him into the Star Dragon so he could better resist the criminal known as Maximus.

Gareth turned in wonder at everything and spotted his old friend, his nemesis across the room surrounded by others that seemed possessed of the same, dark aura. Gareth tried to move, to attack the man, to finally kill him and make the galaxy a safer place, but he found himself held.

"No violence will be allowed, Gareth," *Speaker For The Communion* announced. "*The Communion* alone will *Judge*, and then punishment will be meted out."

Gareth felt terrible psychic fingers reach inside his soul and grope around. He had no other way to describe it. If his brains were a bowl of wet olives, someone was rifling through, looking for that perfect one, presumably to stick on the end of their finger, like everyone did when they had olives to munch. It didn't hurt, but the violation was something he would never forget, even if these people meant no personal animosity.

Still, it was wrong.

"But your intent is plainly known, Gareth," another voice said. "Your instincts will be judged by the outcomes you seek, and not merely the crime of being a human in the *Accord of Souls*."

Gareth turned and the one speaking seemed to be the Chaa known as *Astray in Darkness*. Gareth did not understand the implications of the sigil, but it did not seem as hostile as some of the others. *Mountain*, perhaps. Or *Merciless*.

Another name seemed to be resting behind *Astray in Darkness*. Gareth had the impression of a figurehead on a mighty sailing ship. Except *Astray in Darkness* was beyond even that.

Bowsprit. The closest bit of the ship to the horizon. That was the being's soul. He had gone astray in darkness seeking for something he did not understand. That none of them understood.

Gareth bowed, acknowledging the words and the intent. A human in the *Accord* was the single greatest crime possible. The only solution was dissolution.

Gareth could accept that, if it made the *Accord* safe again. If somehow, humans could be bottled up forever, or at least until they managed to grow up and become responsible, galactic citizens.

However long that might take. The Chaa had already waited fifty thousand years.

"There are two others whose crimes must be weighed first," *Uplifter* spoke next, the rage in his being palpable. "I did not give you art and civilization to have you cast it all away thus. You will face me."

Gareth recognized the forms of Morty and Xiomber. They even seemed to coalesce into their physical bodies as he watched, transforming from ghosts to bodies.

Both wore blue dungarees and T-shirts somehow not dripped on from lunch. They looked around with something approaching fear, but only for a moment before jaws clenched and eyes got all squinty.

"The *Accord of Souls* was designed to provide the greatest benefit for the greatest number of future being, Morty and Xiomber," *Uplifter* growled. "I see in your souls nothing but disdain for others and criminal behavior that leaves me appalled. What defense would you offer?"

Xiomber's snout opened, but no words came out. Morty, however, was having none of it.

"Hey, pal, we've pled guilty," the Yuudixtl scientist snapped. "We're already probably going to spent the rest of our lives in jail, okay? You wanna talk mitigating circumstances, maybe? It ain't all evil around here."

"What could you possibly offer that would offset the crime of bringing the human Marc Sarzynski into *Accord* Space?" *Uplifter* sneered savagely.

Gareth didn't even know gods were capable of that range of emotion, but then he had never met a god before.

"The Star Dragon, pal," Morty's jaw thrust out. "We went looking for a hero, when it became obvious just how badly we'd screwed up. I'd screwed up. How screwed the rest of you were going to be if we didn't do something. And don't give me that crap about us going to the authorities with what I knew, like good, little *Accord* citizens. Grodray and Baker here can tell you just how badly bent the cops were. Not just here, on most worlds. You people should have come back a thousand years ago, if you wanted to fix things quietly."

Gareth felt his blood pool in his stomach with sudden fear. This would be the point where Zeus would have blasted Morty off of Olympus, to fall to his death on the rocks below.

Instead, silence reigned. Awkward, extended silence.

Another voice suddenly broke the silence. *Narrator of History*, if Gareth had memorized them in the correct order.

"The Yuudixlt speaks truth, if rather bluntly and without charm," *Narrator of History* observed in a rich, baritone voice that Gareth would have gladly spent all evening listening to. "We yet bear some responsibility, having fixed the structure the current generation of our descendants has inherited."

That voice reminded him of his dad, telling bedtime stories before tucking Gareth and his brother in. Not that Dad would have even made something like this seem believable. Maybe a radio announcer, tucking all the little boys and girls into bed for the evening with a scientifiction tale, before moving on to play some soft, orchestral jazz as a way to get them to sleep without needing a glass of water in twenty minutes.

"The complexities are so noted," *Speaker For The Communion* announced in a voice that somehow seemed less angry, if no less powerful, to Gareth's weary ear. "All of the *Accord of Souls* can hear us. Every human alive will be made to understand their place, and their fate. This Court is in session. As *Speaker For The Communion*, I will preside, but *The Communion* itself will act as one. *Last Traveler*, you will present your findings that have brought us thus, for the first time in Five Chitra."

CHAA

HE HAD BEEN the last of *The Communion* to depart *Almar*, the *Axle of Time* itself. Not because of any great emotional attachment to the place itself, but so that others could race ahead and hopefully find the trail of the Creator. *First Immortal, Seeker for the Knee of God*, and *Glory in Sunrise* had left first, traversing several of the great wormholes in near space, listening for those echoes that said He had walked this way.

Last Traveler had remained behind nearly a third of a Chitra, watching over the newly-created thing that *Magistrate* and *Uplifter* had created. And perhaps to help the newly sentient species to find their places. The Grace would have eventually found themselves, but he had given them the suggestion to use art in an attempt to resolve their own sensory overload into something that others might understand.

Similarly, the Moisa were builders. Had always been builders. Perhaps *Last Traveler* had offered them architecture as a way of expressing their love of organization and strength.

As the *Last Traveler* to leave, he still looked upon his various descendants as grandchildren. The kind to be both spoiled and educated, as one did. To fire their dreams as well as their intellect.

It had brought him back to *Almar* time and again, just to bask in the glory of what his grandchildren had attained, and continued to explore. The new worlds brought into the *Accord*. The new art. Music. Even titanic, bronze statuary that was currently all the rage with the Grace.

To his many witnesses, *Last Traveler* communicated those visions, those dreams, those memories.

"And then the first seed of darkness bloomed," he said, turning his eye on the human Marc Sarzynski.

Maximus. A killer without hesitation, for whatever bits of remorse yet lived deep in his soul. There was light to be seen there, but even that was cast into service of evil.

He looked into the souls of several witnesses and brought the story forth.

In a galaxy that was not supposed to know crime, somehow the powerful beings of *The Communion* had missed the rise of a new creature called a crime boss.

Cinnra the Warreth had been such a creature. In a galaxy that was supposed to bind peace within the psionic resonance known as the *Accord of Souls*, some people had been born broken. Or somehow achieved it.

Last Traveler understood then that *The Communion* as an entity had failed. They had not foreseen that one could live only partially within *Accord* with one's neighbors. That poverty and want could exist in a galaxy where anything might be within the reach of your dreams. That the Uplifted could still prey upon one another.

He called forth the glyph of Cinnra the Warreth. Crime boss. Deviant. Dominator. But not a killer. Cinnra had determined that he needed a killer, in order to fortify his hold on a criminal underworld that was yet filled mostly with only-partially-broken souls.

He had tasked his best scientists with finding such a creature. They had located a human. Marc Sarzynski. And caused him to be brought to the worlds of the *Accord of Souls*.

Last Traveler was a compassionate being, filled with love and affection for *Those Left Behind*, including the ones he was not directly related to. The other sixteen clans.

He still felt a growl bubble up as a glyph that encompassed the two Yuudixtl criminals. The two had the courtesy to bow before his rage. Mitigation later they might have attempted, but the original sin was still theirs to own.

"These two bear that mark," *Last Traveler* said. "For their own arrogant motives, their own chance at a form of legend, of godhead, they brought Marc Sarzynski forth. This crime is not in dispute."

"No, pal, it is not," the angrier of the two, Morty, somehow managed to glyph back at him, although none but *The Communion* might hear it.

"Maximus, in due course, overthrew Cinnra the Warreth, killed him, and took over his gang, slaying many who would not bow to an alien, even one that would now pass as Vanir to the casual glance. One now may witness his crimes."

Last Traveler pulled forth many glyphs for evidence, as Maximus was a stain on all of civilization and everyone here needed to appreciate the depths of depravity to which a human might delve. Murder. Torture. Kidnapping. Extortion. Corruption of the Body Public and Politic.

All these things were shown to the assembled witnesses, *The Communion*, even those of the *Ascended Chaa* who chose to watch.

"And there are others," he spoke once the glyph had passed.

Zorge the Nari. Maiair the Warreth. Yooyar the Warreth. Mishalska the Nari. Other faces not present, but that was either because they had been captured and awaited their punishment, or had not accompanied Maximus to *Earth*.

Now *Last Traveler* showed a series of human faces that he extracted from the minds of the criminals. Demian O'Rourke, a human crime boss. Four other men who served the human, as well as a young woman of no great note, other than to want to belong.

"I could go on," *Last Traveler* said. "Without the Accord to bind them into peace, humans are just as dangerous, just as violent as we had expected them to be, seven Chitra ago when the vote was taken to exclude them from our construction."

"Members of *The Communion*, how do you vote?" *Speaker For The Communion* asked the assembled gods.

Each submitted a glyph, democracy being the only way to truly organize such a construct, where twelve powerful beings who might live forever did not wish to take permanent responsibility.

Quickly, the lopsided natures of things became clear.

"So it has been decided," *Speaker For The Communion* announced in a voice that even the ephemeral beings could hear. "The Earth and all of the humans are to be expunged. Thus will the *Accord of Souls* be protected, while not tasking any of the *Ascended Chaa* with having to watch over them and prevent their escape into the larger galaxy. *Merciless* has demanded responsibility for destroying humanity. If none would dispute that, he will now act."

"No," a voice rose out of the midst of the assembled watchers.

Last Traveler was shocked at the vehemence of the tone, especially coming from a young Grace woman. He could see one of the many humans wanting to rage, but this person surprised him.

"Speak, Ilak Vorta," *Last Traveler* commanded.

He had been granted the floor to present his case, and had done so, unaware that there might rise a defender. He would hear her testimony.

She turned to face him and pulled from her head a fine, silk cloth that had been obscuring her sensory tentacles. From the gasps around her, *Last Traveler* determined that only half of the humans were surprised that a Grace walked among them, disguised.

"If you act thus, you are no better than they are,"

she snarled in a tight, angry voice that almost caused *Last Traveler* to flounder back a step.

He looked within the woman briefly, and then within himself and saw the problem.

She was right.

GRACE

FATIMA KNEW that she appeared human to the men and women around her, including Royston, Pippa, and Hank. Even the ones that knew better.

The human musician Fatima somehow knew was named Ellen had understood that Fatima was something more. Fatima Darzi was only an identity she had assumed, in order to walk safely among the humans.

More safely. They were still the most violent, most dangerous species ever to achieve technology, according to the records, however ancient.

And yet, she had gone among them willingly. Met many humans, across the entire spectrum of behaviors and personalities. Had been accepted as one of them, with no more threat to her person than perhaps Sir West's towering indignation that Royston hadn't called the man and let him know they were in London.

Fatima picked Sir West out of the crowd from where he had been trying to slink to a corner, invisible as a mouse attempting to hide from the giants.

"So it has been decided," *Speaker For The Communion* commanded a death sentence on an entire species. "The Earth and all of the humans are to be expunged. Thus will the *Accord of Souls* be protected, while not tasking any of the *Ascended Chaa* with having to watch over them and prevent their escape into the larger galaxy. *Merciless* has demanded responsibility for destroying humanity. If none would dispute that, he will now act."

"No," the word exploded out of her lips before she could stop it.

One of the Great Ones turned to her now.

"Speak, Ilak Vorta," he commanded.

She was a spy, not an orator, but somehow, it was her rage that let her break through the fear that threatened to smother all these other beings that had been brought here to witness the Chaa known as *The Communion*.

"If you act thus, you are no better than they are," the phrase erupted from her like a volcano suddenly awakening.

"Why say you thus?" one of the others called down to her.

Fatima turned and glared back at the tremendous menace emanating from the one that she had heard called *Merciless*.

He glyphed her now, and she understood how he came to take this name, when he had been someone else before.

Fatima watched history unfold as the *Ascended Chaa* traveled the width and breadth of this galaxy in their quest to find evidence of He Who Created All.

Watched them encounter another species like the humans, tucked in a distant corner of the spiral, almost across the Core from Earth.

Six worlds colonized from the seventh. Warlike. Violent. Xenophobic as they wiped out a planet where the natives were just beginning to understand stone tools.

They were perhaps the most dangerous element in the galaxy, while the *Ascended Chaa* were as yet only a collection of philosophers and seekers. Until *The Communion* spoke.

Fatima watched these same beings pronounce doom on the Tronafora. Watched the being who took the new glyph of *Merciless*, as he hunted down every ship, every creature, every bit of evidence that the Tronafora ever existed. Seven stars cast into sudden supernova stage by the violent expedient of dropping a black hole singularity into close proximity.

Seven star systems wiped clean of all life.

"Yes," Fatima agreed. "You have the power to destroy. And the will to commit xenocide. But you have not given the humans any chance to learn."

"They cannot learn better," one of the other sneered at her. "Look at Marc Sarzynski and tell me his is capable of civilized behavior."

"He is at the far end of human behavior," Fatima snapped back at the god. At all the gods "There are twelve billion others you could choose to study instead."

"And we would find the same capability for violence," that woman(?) called back. "The same murderous rages. The same disdain for helping their fellow creatures in need."

"You would find that walking the streets of

Orgoth Vortai," Fatima sneered back in a similar tone. "You would also destroy all the amazing things that humans are capable of achieving."

Fatima tried to glyph back to them, as *Merciless* had done, but lacked the understanding of how such a thing was done. Perhaps she also lacked the power, but her rage would not be stilled.

"Allow me?" a new voice appeared in her head.

Astray in Darkness held out a hand, at least metaphorically. She took it and felt the Chaa reach into her mind and grasp at those things Fatima wanted these angry gods to see.

Art. Ancient architecture from her putative homeland of Persia. Music of the souq and the bandstand. Even American cooking, almost as bland and boring as English, but then she threw in Thai, Cameroonian, and Ecuadorian food, just to show them the range of humanity.

All of these images, these glyphs, *Astray in Darkness* lifted up and cast into the sky for her, like soap bubbles in a soft breeze.

"Thank you," Fatima bowed to the Chaa.

He surprised her by returning the bow.

Fatima turned the other way, scanning the crowd of beings until she found the one she wanted.

Ellen, the singer, had ended up not far from Royston, Pippa, and Crown Prince Henry, in disguise tonight as merely Hank, but still the man who would be King of England one day. Fatima tried to convey a smile to them, but she focused her attention on Ellen.

She had not known the woman's name until now, as the musical group went by a vague appellation that included no personal names. But she was Ellen. Her own glyph was nearly as bright as Royston's.

Perhaps only Gareth's and Maximus' shown brighter, among the two score of humans who had been gathered up.

"I need your help," Fatima explained as she walked (floated?) over to the woman.

"Mine?" Ellen replied, stunned.

"Yours was the power that showed Royston how to achieve the higher physics and mathematics he needed, in order to understand how to step across space/time," Fatima said. "I need you to explain it to them."

Fatima gesture encompassed the twelve beings, but also included all the other species that made up the *Accord of Souls*, including herself.

"Explain?" Ellen asked.

"Your music," Fatima said. "I have never encountered anything with such power. It is a human thing that none but perhaps these gods have ever heard. And even they may be surprised."

"My band isn't here," Ellen said, turning this way and that to spy the crowd.

Fatima cursed under her breath. The Chaa had gathered together beings of power and importance, but not recognized the gestalt that this woman contained when she was up on that stage.

"Can you bring her band here?" Fatima turned to *Astray in Darkness* and asked.

It was a silly question. These creatures had stopped time and opened up and closed portals to a dozen worlds in order to gather this assembly. *Merciless* was prepared to pick up a black hole with one hand and drop it into the orbit of the human planet *Mercury*, in order to disrupt Earth's sun permanently.

"Why?" one of the angrier gods challenged.

"Because you do not understand," Royston suddenly appeared at her side.

Fatima could taste the rage boiling off the man as he took her hand and held it, almost as if it was the most natural thing in the world.

Like kissing him had been.

"Because I could not have achieved what I did without the power of this woman and her friends," Royston challenged them all loudly. "You need to feel that, experience it, and it is not enough to pick it up out of my memory and try to experience it second-hand."

Fatima felt rougher hands take hold of her mind, sifting it for what Royston knew. A moment later, they moved on, and she could tell that they moved on to the man by the way his breath caught.

Finally, Ellen felt the power, the intrusion of a dozen gods in her mind. Fatima reached out with her other hand and found Ellen's. Held it. Let the woman squeeze painfully while the gods ransacked her.

The Chaa withdrew after another moment.

"What says *The Communion*?" the most powerful voice asked.

"I would hear them," *Astray in Darkness* said quietly. "If their species is to end shortly, perhaps we owe them that much courtesy. Each of us will stand before *He Who Created All* at some future date. Each of us will have the stain of destroying the Tronafora on our souls, even if only one actually acted. *The Communion* still decided upon xenocide as a body. We all share that crime."

Fatima watched as the others were swayed by

that logic, until all seemed to favor it. Even *Merciless* nodded.

Between one heartbeat and the next, a stage appeared. Five men in identical, black suits stood upon it, holding human instruments that Fatima still found esoteric and strange, but as with all things human, there was an edge of wildness that the *Accord of Souls* could not fathom.

Could not grasp.

"What the hell?" one of the guitarists murmured as he was suddenly transported from a darkened auditorium to the metaphorical hall of *The Communion*.

Ellen was still holding her hand, so the woman pulled Fatima enough to turn her back.

"I do not understand," Ellen said in a simple voice. "What do you need?"

"They do not believe," a new voice intruded.

Fatima turned to see Prince Hank suddenly close. Focused. Intent. Looking so much older than fifteen years in his poise and stance.

"It is like it was with my mother, Sir West, and Sir William," the young man said. "They had heard the stories, but discounted them. Sir William even went so far as to suggest that we summon you to the palace, in an effort to replicate it or prove Dr. Loughty wrong. That would have failed, for all the reasons that Ms. Darzi was right about and they were wrong. I was wrong. We need you, all of you. We need you to explain to these beings, these gods I suppose, what it means to be human."

"Who are you?" Ellen asked sharply.

Fatima smiled. Unlike the Americans she had met, Ellen was English, at least by her accent. Fatima only sounded Persian, because she needed to. She could speak English better than perhaps most of the people here. Or drift into any of the regional creoles necessary to hide among them.

"Henry Windsor," Hank introduced himself. "Crown Prince of England. Son of Queen Elizabeth III."

"Oh, shit," Ellen gasped. "Really?"

Fatima found it amusing that Ellen rounded on Royston at that.

"This is who you brought to hear me?" Ellen demanded angrily.

"No," Royston smiled in a way both serious and serene. "I brought Fatima to hear you. Hank was a necessary accompaniment because otherwise his mother might have insisted that you play the Palace. That was exactly the sort of situation I was hoping to avoid, but that is out of our hands now."

"Most of the people in here won't understand," Ellen tried to counter.

"Most of them won't matter, Ellen," Fatima said, gesturing. "Those twelve are the ones you need to reach."

"With music?" Ellen asked.

"With the power of rock and roll," Royston explained. "Like you did for me that first time, when you showed me the true music of the spheres, and how to unravel them."

"I'm not sure I can," Ellen faltered.

"I just witnessed you doing it," Fatima said. "I know what you are capable of."

ALIEN

GARETH FINALLY COULD MOVE, as long as he did not stray in the direction of Marc Sarzynski and his small band of criminal aliens. The ones Gareth had been coming to arrest, or destroy, leading Jackeith Grodray and Eveth Baker through a wormhole to *Earth*.

At the same time, he could not bring himself to place even a single foot in the direction he really wanted to go. Towards her.

This was what cowardice felt like. Gareth had never known it. Had never encountered a thing that caused him to retire and refrain. Even dating a volleyball player a foot taller than he was had been merely an adventure for an ambitious thirteen-year-old.

But he could not approach. Could not move.

Fortunately(?) she was not so inhibited.

Gareth watched Pippa detach herself from Royston and a Grace woman who had somehow become the speaker for the humans.

Pippa.

In his pocket, Gareth still had the ring he had been holding in his hands at the moment when destiny intruded. When Morty and Xiomber reached across the width of the galaxy, because they needed a hero if they were going to save the *Accord* from Marc.

But he could not move. Could not rush to her. Take her in his arms and feel he heart surely pounding as hard as his was.

She approached slowly. Almost timidly, like a forest creature who had never seen a man before and how no understanding of how dangerous they were.

But it was still Pippa. Still the woman he loved. Still the face that haunted him when he tried to sleep.

"Gareth?" she whispered as she got close.

He nodded, unable to even breathe lest this all be a soap bubble that would pop and evaporate before his eyes, like so many other dreams had been.

Gareth felt a hand on his back suddenly. It shoved, and he staggered forward a step before he could catch himself.

Gareth looked back and saw the tremendous grin form on Talyarkinash's face as her whiskers flared out and her ears seemed to scan the skies.

"Hi," he managed as he turned back to Pippa, unsure what to say or do.

And then she was in his arms, crying and hiccupping.

It felt so strange, holding her. He had been six foot two the last time he had seen her, then only a head taller than she. Now, she barely came up to the middle of his Vanir chest.

But he cried. And laughed. And held her tight, unsure if he would ever see her again.

"What are you now?" she finally asked, after they both managed to breathe.

"A Vanir," Gareth responded. "It was the closest form Morty and Xiomber could find for a renegade human, when they transformed Marc, so they did the same to me. At first."

"The little lizardman called you a Star Dragon, Gareth," she murmured.

Around them, the world went on, but he had eyes only for Pippa.

"That was the second part, Pippa," he whispered. "When I needed a tool that could stand against Marc. Could overawe his criminals. When I needed to be a symbol for all of the *Accord*."

"So you are truly a dragon?" she asked, shock resounding in her voice.

"I can become one, yes," Gareth said. "Talyarkinash helped with that part."

Gareth reached back and snagged the Nari woman by the arm before she could react.

"Pippa Loughty, it is my great pleasure to introduce you to one of my closest friends in the *Accord of Souls*, Dr. Talyarkinash Liamssen," he said. "Talyarkinash, the woman you've heard me talk so much about. *Pippa*."

It was interesting, watching the two of them shake hands. Gareth had spent so much time around Nari, Grace, and Vanir that a human like Pippa appeared alien to his eyes.

"Gareth saved my life," Talyarkinash smiled. "I am so glad to be able to finally meet you. To thank you for making him such a wonderful person."

"Me?" Pippa was shocked.

"You," Talyarkinash said. "Let nobody lead you

astray on this, but he has been pining for you, loyal to you, from the very first moment I met him. Everything he has done, after what was necessary to save the *Accord*, was with an eye towards somehow transforming himself back into a human so he could return home, if the authorities would allow it."

"Why would they not?" Pippa asked, her eyes going back and forth.

"Because I know too much," Gareth said. "I have had to study everything I could of the *Accord* in order to try and join the Constabulary, the police forces of the *Accord* that are just like Earth Force Sky Patrol. Humans are not supposed to know anything about the *Accord*, for reasons around us that are obvious."

"He even proposed kidnapping you, knowing that the two of you would never be able to return home afterwards, Pippa," Talyarkinash said. "Just so that you could be happy together."

"Would they have allowed that?" Pippa gasped.

"I don't know," Gareth felt his shoulders come up automatically. "We had to stop Maximus from conquering the galaxy first. That would have been later."

"Will we even survive?" Pippa asked. "Father knew there were aliens, that's how he unmasked Fatima as a Grace, but these being seem to be so much more powerful."

"They are the most powerful of the Chaa," Gareth nodded. "The ones who created the *Accord of Souls*. Who uplifted Talyarkinash's ancestors to intelligence and civilization. Marc and I represent the worst crimes imaginable, just by existing in the *Accord*."

"Father found out how you had vanished," Pippa smiled. "His experiments back-tracked what the two little lizardmen did. That's why Fatima came to us, to see what he knew, and if it could be derailed."

"I doubt that it could have," Gareth said. "Humans are too inquisitive."

"That's what Father said," Pippa nodded. "The best that could happen would be if he could least Sky Patrol astray for six months by claiming that something was wrong with the math. Then we went looking for the leaders of the *Accord of Souls* to ask them what could be done."

Gareth could not suppress the gasp that escaped him. How much had he missed, spending all his time trying to fight crime in this alien place?

"What happened?" Talyarkinash came to his rescue.

"We went out into the Arizona desert," Pippa explained. "Fatima stepped through a portal and went…somewhere. When she came back, it became our mission to find the woman Ellen and her band, so that Fatima could see what had happened."

"I don't understand," Gareth managed to squeeze out of the tension in his chest.

How close was the Chaa to just destroying everything? What could he do to somehow convince them to save all the innocents, even if they had to punish him for merely existing?

"Father thinks that it was only the combination of his brilliance and the woman's music that opened the pathways in his mind," Pippa said. "Perhaps without him and her, humanity would still require centuries before they developed the technology to find the aliens. We went out into the desert originally, in case the alien overlords decided that they needed to kill us, to stop things."

"Suicide?" Talyarkinash asked in a shocked, hollow voice.

"Sacrifice," Pippa corrected her. "Our lives, for the rest of humanity, if that was what was necessary. Nobody else knew, or perhaps even guessed that semi-benevolent aliens might be involved in Gareth's disappearance. That they might be watching us."

"And the musician?" Gareth asked. "Where does she fit in all this?"

"I took Father to see her and her band perform in London," Pippa said, still holding on to him with one hand. "Her music is simply impossible to describe, other than to call it the most powerful, most emotional thing I have ever heard. By listening to it,Father found the pathways to higher mathematics."

Gareth turned to Talyarkinash with a question on his face, but no words to express his need.

"It makes perfect sense to me, Gareth," she explained. "Humans have a powerful, latent, psionic ability. That's what you tap in order to transform, and to fly. Her father has similar capabilities for pure mental ability. This other human must express herself through her music."

Before Gareth could answer, a bright light filled the space where all the ghosts and gods were standing. One end of the auditorium was suddenly a raised platform, a stage, with five human men, dressed in skinny, black suits and holding instruments, standing around confused and concerned.

CRIMINAL

MARC STUDIED the room as his senses cleared. He had been holding a pistol in one hand, knelt behind a table that would provide some modicum of cover when the Constables came through their portal, but he had nothing now. Not a beam, not a knife. Nothing.

Maiair and Yooyar were the closest, standing on either side of him like bodyguards. Zorge was just ahead on his right. Glancing back, Mishalska and Two-gun Kowalski were behind him, watching his back, at least as much as they could.

O'Rourke and his people were in a second cluster. Not close, but not clear across the space, like the Chaa had picked everyone up and then put them down in a pattern.

Marc had heard about the Chaa. Some of his gang had been extremely superstitious when he took over, but Marc had thinned those ranks pretty quickly. Religion was nice, and a useful way to bilk suckers, but people concerned about going to hell for what they've done have a tendency to have second thoughts in the current world.

Eventually, enough of them would break under the stress and throw themselves on the mercies of the nearest priest. Which, in turn, usually meant a call to the cops, and a raid, possibly a shootout.

The rationalists had generally been the ones Marc kept.

Who in his right might expected to be called to the carpet by literal gods? And that was what Marc was looking at today.

There had been enough jokes in the gang. How bad could their activities be if the Chaa hadn't come back to stop them, after all?

Until they did. So maybe it had gotten bad enough. And maybe Marc was facing Hell finally, when he had expected it to be much farther off in his future.

He found he could not move in the direction of Gareth or those other two Vanir Constables: Grodray and Baker. Hopefully, they couldn't come over here. He had only a handful of his people, desperately outnumbered by the rest of the room, even before Dankworth turned into that damnable dragon.

And none of the androids were here. Marc assumed at this point that one of those twelve gods had understood what the machines were and simply annihilated them. It was what they should have done.

"What the hell is going on?" Two-Gun murmured from behind him.

"You know most of what I do, Two-Gun," Marc turned enough to answer. "Other than these are apparently the gods who originally created the *Accord of Souls* fifty thousand years ago."

"Gods?" the gangster asked with a growl. "Like Zeus and them?"

"Close enough for our purposes," Marc replied. "Ultimately powerful beings who aren't going to like us one bit for meddling in their sand box."

"I got no guns," Two-Gun muttered. "No knife. Nothing."

"Same here," Marc said. "They wanted us all in one room, it looks like, so they could judge us all."

"He said all of Earth was listening in," Two-Gun's voice took on a measure of broken awe now. "Is that even possible?"

"You tell me what limitations gods have and I'll tell you, Two-Gun," Marc snapped back.

"Crap, we're doomed."

"Probably," Mark said in a softer voice. "But we're going down fighting if we have to. I'd rather explain to Lucifer that it took a dozen gods to kill me, than to politely let those people line me up against the wall and stick a cigarette in my mouth."

Maiair's hand found his and squeezed. Marc drew some comfort from that. She wasn't his first choice for true love, but this woman probably understood him better than most. The one he would have chosen was over there, grinding salt into yet another wound, because that one had also chosen Gareth.

Marc was willing to grant that he had driven Talyarkinash into the man's arms. Stabbing a woman and threatening to cut her throat was not the way to any woman's heart.

But she had chosen to betray him when Morty

and Xiomber came to her. She could have just as easily called Marc then and had his goons come over and rescue her.

He tried moving towards O'Rourke, to offer them some explanation and encouragement, but suddenly found his way blocked, almost as if his feet had been nailed to the floor.

One of the gods seemed to shine a light on him from their spot up on the dais.

"You will remain still, Marc Sarzynski," the being said. "We will get to you in good time."

COP

ANEN WARDSON FELT a surge of pride as she watched the agent known to the humans as Fatima Darzi step up and challenged the Chaa. Anen had sent the Grace woman to *Earth* to find a way to prevent this very tragedy, if possible. That Fatima had failed was not something that should weigh heavily on her conscience.

After all, they had all failed.

Very shortly, *The Communion* was likely to wipe out all the humans in existence, which would probably include Gareth Dankworth. Losing him would be a shame, because the man really had worked to redeem himself, but Anen did not expect gods like these to understand something so simple as that.

She turned and found Petim close. She found it interesting that, of all of the *Accord* Commissioners, only Petim had been brought here. She would have expected them to bring everyone when they brought her, but perhaps the one known as *Last Traveler* had understood already that Petim was the Commission, as far as that went. His will would carry the rest.

That they had also picked up the First Inspector of the Constabulary from that meeting meant that they still needed something from her.

Anen had no idea what she might contribute to such a decision. She had been trying to find a way to save the humans from themselves, right up until the moment when it became clear that Marc Sarzynski had made it to Earth. That had sealed his fate, and all of his kin, because there was no way except death to prevent an army of humans from coming through a wormhole one of these days and attacking *Accord* worlds. Whose death was just a matter of scale.

And nothing the *Accord* Constabulary could have done would have stopped them except to slaughter Sarzynski and his gang, and bring back the corpses for confirmation. Otherwise, it would have been a war.

Certainly, Vanir were physically more impressive figures, compared to the humans. But everyone would still be possessed of utter terror to confront a renegade human, especially an armed one. Prime Inspectors like Jack Grodray or Eveth Baker might not hesitate, but too many others would, and it would get them killed.

Even now, she had a hard time even contemplating taking a single step in the direction of the man who had brought them all to this point.

No, that wasn't fair.

Marc Sarzynski had brought them all here. Royston Loughty had merely been trying to solve a mystery, and accidentally uncovered a conspiracy instead. That he had found a way to open his own wormholes had only brought things to her attention, in time for the Constabulary to chase Sarzynski as far as Earth.

And to prepare to destroy all the humans.

Her methods wouldn't have been as comprehensive as the Chaa intended, but nobody knew a way to call on the gods and get them to listen.

Except that now they were here, and going to commit xenocide. While she watched.

There had to be a better solution. Anen had bet Fatima's life on finding it.

Perhaps she should have bet her own.

That thought broke her free from the stasis that had held her in place. She didn't want to think of it as cowardice, right as that might be. She needed to put her badge first now, and not her xenophobia.

She was a cop. Humans didn't know any better, for the most part. Gareth Dankworth did, and that knowledge just drove him to be as good a cop as he could manage, doing anything Jack or Baker had asked without questions.

That pushed her foot forward another step.

She quickly found herself standing next to Dr. Loughty and Fatima, even as something changed and the room was suddenly an auditorium, with a fresh crop of humans, all male, all dressed alike, all musicians, if she understood Darzi's reports correctly.

"Dr. Loughty, we have not met," she said as the man turned towards her, hoping that the Chaa had done something to let him understand her, even though they spoke different languages normally. "I am Anen Wardson, First Inspector of the

Constabulary. Gareth Dankworth works for me now."

She got the impression that her much greater size did not intimidate the man in the slightest as he looked up at her. He was a human, so perhaps not.

A moment later, his face broke into a grin.

"First Inspector, thank you for sending Fatima," he said in a strange tone. "We have all tried to salvage the situation, but none have risked more than she. Please remember that when the rest of us are gone and blame and favor needs to be apportioned accordingly."

"You expect to die shortly?" Anen asked, shocked at the calm way the human seemed to accept his fate.

These monsters should have been fighting tooth and nail like crazed beasts, rather than philosophically accepting things.

"Madame, I have been living with that expectation since the moment that the Sector Marshal aboard The Arsenal told me that the niece of my old friend, Firuz Alinejad, wished to study physics with me," Loughty smiled calmly. "I had known Fatima Darzi when she was much younger. Given the circumstances, she could only be an imposter, but even then I had no idea how deep I might find turtles if I went seeking."

Anen wasn't sure she understood the reference, a cultural thing, but she got the gist of it. Royston Loughty was far more canny than anyone had given him credit for. And braver than she imagined, to simply continue on with what he was doing, trying to find a way to save things, even if it might cost him his life.

Should have cost him his life.

Was eventually going to.

Anen understood now more of what made Gareth Dankworth who he was. The unstoppable drive to make the galaxy a better place, even as he found himself trapped in a distant land and unable to return home.

Gareth had not even paused in his efforts, merely pivoted and turned himself into an Art Fraud specialist, working in a culture he had never imagined a year ago, because Jack Grodray had asked.

Yes, Gareth Dankworth was a cop. And Royston Loughty seemed to have something of that as well, even as he was closer in age to her than the youngsters in this room and was known to her as a scientist.

But they shared a glance and Anen knew. Yes. Royston Loughty had been an Earth Force Sky Patrol agent at some point. Something like Fatima, so deep undercover that nobody else in the room, except perhaps a dozen gods, knew the truth besides her.

Fatima and the other human turned to them now.

"Rock and roll?" the stranger asked one last time.

"It will be the greatest concert ever played," Loughty turned back to the woman and said calmly. "Not just the finest you ever play, but the most powerful thing ever recorded, because there are several thousand gods around us listening today."

The woman gasped.

"Thousands," she squeaked.

"Look around you," Loughty smiled. "You can see them, smiling back from the edges of the room. They are waiting for you, and you alone."

Anen could not see them when she glanced, but

she also was part of the *Accord of Souls*, that psionic entity defined by the binding that brought seventeen species together into one.

It also excluded the humans, by design.

Perhaps, fifty thousand years ago, the Chaa had understood what these upstarts would be capable of turning into.

Or would become, had they survived.

ROCKER

ELLEN HAD NEVER WANTED MORE from life than to be able to stand up on that stage and sing, then go home and hide from the world when she was done. People didn't frighten her so much as exhaust her with trying to keep up with their unconscious communications.

She didn't understand it, most of the time. Doctors had called her a mid-functioning introvert. Any more so, and they might have prescribed drugs to *fix* her, had she let them, but Ellen knew she never would stoop to that level.

Fixing her involved taking away the one thing that gave her purpose.

Music.

She could impersonate normal enough of the time, but only in a world gone completely black and white, when she normally lived in such a rich sensorium that frequently it wanted to overwhelm her.

And then this strange woman held her hand.

Ellen had been consciously ignoring the fact that the stranger from the auditorium was a medusa, with tentacles instead of hair. Royston didn't seem to mind, so that must make it okay.

Right?

But Fatima held her hand, and suddenly Ellen felt her own power embrace the stranger.

Grace. That was what she was. Ellen smiled with understanding on so many levels.

Grace.

Every one of those tentacles was another set of eyes, nose, and ear, sifting the world around her constantly and feeding Fatima so much information that she must be mad. Except she wasn't.

She lived in a place where everyone else was black and white. Two dimensional.

Mundane.

"I'm not sure I can," Ellen tried to explain to all these people that the power wasn't hers to command.

"I just witnessed you doing it," Fatima replied with such surety of purpose that Ellen felt the ground grow solid beneath their feet.. "I know what you are capable of."

Yes, she probably did. Nobody else in this room would understand what it meant, to be subject to so many details constantly. To be unable to block them out, because anything she tried would drop a solid, glass wall three feet thick between Ellen and the rest of the universe.

But the Grace lived with that every day. Ellen could taste it as her powers touched Fatima's mind.

Ellen mastered her own soul and thrust herself into the ritual that carried her onto that stage each night. The deep breaths, counting by fives. The way she could push everything backwards four point seven three yards so they couldn't touch her.

In her mind, she turned the entire stage dark. Forced her audience to exist in shadows so they were nothing more than a suggestion of eyes reflecting at the edge of the fire.

Not people. Not watching her.

Not stealing her life energy, even as she was giving it away with as much effort as she could manage.

Ellen nodded to Fatima and let go of her hand.

The world turned a little more gray around her, but she could manage that.

She wasn't alone in the universe. She had the Grace to remember.

Even if the Gods were finally going to take their gift back and cast her forever into the hell of noise and madness.

Ellen blew out her breath and stepped up on the platform to stand before her band.

As always, she stopped seeing them as people. They became extensions of herself. There were no words to describe it, but she could tell what each of the men was thinking, as if it was printed on his tie.

Tommy, Lead Guitar, desperately worried about her, but putting on a brave face of the detached, rock guitarist, to provide her a platform she could grasp when the cold, dark waters she swam threatened to be too much.

Dave on Rhythm Guitar, set to hold the melody in place, regardless of what any of the rest of the universe thought they might do.

Mick on the upright bass, prepared to call forth all the hosts of Hell with his playing, an earthquake in his fingertips even now as he studied the very Gods around them and challenged them to meet his beat.

Rhys, surrounded by that tremendously-oversized drum set, from which he could give you almost anything if you let him know ahead of time the sound you needed.

Dalton, a ragtime, boogie-woogie pianist who could have played before kings and any classical conductor in the world, if he didn't want to rock.

They grounded her. Gave her peace. Forced her to breathe.

Ellen found the microphone just as she had left it five minutes ago.

Or a lifetime.

At her feet, a single piece of paper with a list of words. Dave always penciled in the set list after sitting perfectly still and watching her for ten minutes when they first got into the green room. Somehow, he could absorb her needs and flow, just right.

Every time.

This set had been perfect for London. For Royston, whom she had known would be there, and needing something special from them.

She would have to top it.

Ellen bent and picked up the paper, turning to Dave with a question on her face.

"I had two," he said quietly, almost apologetically as he handed her a replacement and took the old one. "Something told me that I needed a second list, as if we were suddenly going to play a whole other concert right after the first one. It made no sense to me three hours ago, but I did it anyway."

No, it wouldn't. How could any of them

understand that they were a single, psionic entity when they played?

Until she had met a God, Ellen hadn't understood.

Until.

Quickly, she scanned Dave's alternate list.

Yes. This was almost identical to the one she had played for Royston the first time they touched across the darkness. When he had need, and she had power, and they had ascended the heavens together.

When they called out to the Gods for knowledge.

And somebody answered.

Ellen pushed her fears to the back of the stage and made them go away. The only thing they could do right now was infect her boys and make them play badly.

She would not allow it.

Ellen turned to Dave and placed his second list beside her microphone stand with a nod. Quickly, Dave pulled out a set of three by five cards and handed them out to the boys.

Royston needed her to go higher than she had ever touched before. Needed her to call down these ancient Godlike beings and demand that they sit quietly while she taught them what it meant to be human.

To be alive.

To be young.

SCIENTIST

ROYSTON WATCHED Fatima communicate with the young woman on a plane of existence he hadn't even understood existed, until he met the first of the beings who had *Ascended.*

Until he met a God.

Royston's soul was just small enough that he had to look around until he found Sir West, still trying to hide at the fringe of this strange mob. Trying to wrap science around everything that had happened.

There are more things in heaven and Earth, Horatio, than are dreamt of in your philosophy.

Human science was insufficient, just as Pippa had suggested to him before, when her pithy observation first drove him to consider rock and roll instead. *Accord* science, with all the magical wonder he had been able to somehow absorb from the corporeal beings around him, was not sufficient.

But now he was dealing with gods. *Ascended Chaa* who had somehow reached a stage of mental development that could not be explained, save to say that humans apparently held that same seed of potential greatness in their collective soul.

If he could find a way to keep these vengeful gods from ending everything tonight.

The room fell silent. Perhaps the entire universe, as *Speaker For The Communion* had said that every human in the Solar System would hear this *Judgment*. The *Accord of Souls* would likewise be poised on the edge of their seats, to have the Chaa themselves return in their lifetime.

Most would not appreciate that only the gravest risk possible would compel such an event, but they would understand the costs tomorrow, after they watched their Gods destroy an entire species.

The scientist in him would miss the chance to explore what would change in their culture from having been here today. Having witnesses the darkness that accompanied godhead.

"What is rock and roll?" the First Inspector, Anen, asked him in a quiet, nervous voice.

Royston took her hand in his and tried to press his understanding towards her with whatever psychic power he apparently possessed. It seemed impossible to describe, but that was because he lacked the vocabulary necessary, that of the gods themselves, to do any better.

"Power," Royston said simply, never relinquishing his hold on Fatima with his other hand.

Royston, the most scientific of minds, holding hands with two alien women and listening to rock and roll. Enjoying it, even.

Who would have imagined?

And then words were unnecessary. The man standing at the battered, wooden upright piano slid a hand down from the top of the scale to draw all mesmerized eyes to the keys.

Royston was prepared for the pulse of energy that seemed to emerge from the woman on the stage as the man began to play. Except that such a word did not do the act justice. As before, he attacked the keyboard as though mortal combat had begun.

Perhaps it had, and this would be the battlefield of choice.

Hard, rhythmic, almost *bombastic*. Here was a man who could challenge Rachmaninoff himself, bringing all that technique and experience to rock and roll instead.

The rhythm guitarist joined in, setting a basic melody in a way Royston hadn't understood, that first night. Such a simple progression of chords, yet it felt almost like a tiler laying a mosaic floor that would somehow vanish beneath your feet, until the moment you stopped when a child noticed it and pointed down with glee at the images.

A full measure later, the other man taught these assembled gods, perhaps the entire universe, the meaning of *Lead Guitar* with a power and emotion that Royston had only known the best violinists and saxophonists to achieve. At least until Pippa had suggested rock and roll might be the solution.

The pulse of energy was like a squall line had emerged from the stage and washed over the entire audience, a tide pushing them a little closer to shore, before the rip currents that would suck them back out to sea.

And then Ellen opened her mouth and sang.

That first night, he hadn't known what to expect. Jazz was famous for scat singers with technical excellence, or torch singers bringing their languid tales of woe to wring your heart.

Ellen was a rocker.

But more than that. She was power. Raw and unrestrained. Anger and love, sophistication and destruction.

It was like the ancient Hindu goddess Kali-ma stood before him on the stage, proclaiming the end of the world.

Considering the company, perhaps it was appropriate. She was facing the end of the world and challenging the gods themselves to stand before her and do their worst.

Royston hoped it would be enough.

SECTOR MARSHAL

IT WAS the worst feeling in the world, to be utterly powerless and to know it. Sector Marshal Alvin Siddall commanded the Earth Force Sky Patrol base known as The Arsenal, located in the L2 LaGrange Point.

The Far Side of the Moon.

Where experiments with dangerous energies or exotic weapons might not destroy the Earth. At least without destroying Luna first. And if they managed that, hadn't they already sealed their fate?

On the main screen, someone, somehow, had caused an image to appear. Alvin already knew that none of his men could control that screen, even as they still had basic control of the base itself.

It was like some alien being demanding that they witness what was happening, frightening as *THAT* concept was.

What was happening?

Alvin could see figures in a large auditorium, almost like a gymnasium in size. Perhaps a hundred lesser shapes, some of which he knew were friends, while the rest were those beings Royston had warned him about.

Aliens. At least a dozen different shapes and sizes, from a medusa to lizardman a stone giant. It was like the ancient Professor had brought his fanciful stories of elves and orcs to life in the modern age.

At the edges of the screen, the appearance of the dozen creatures that had assembled that congress to witness. Alvin had felt the glyph for *The Communion*, as well as their individual names, even across whatever distance existed or didn't between the Arsenal and the Apocalypse.

"Anything on scanners?" Alvin called to the room.

"Negative, sir," one of the men yelled back, face down over an imaging projectors. "All space appears clear to a distance of four light seconds. *Arizona-Seven* is currently returning to Headquarters at L1 under emergency regulations."

"Who has control of the main projection screen?" Alvin asked the room.

"Working at it sir," another man called. "We have all other screens under our control, except…stand by. Sir, engineering reports that at least one screen in every chamber on the Arsenal is currently tuned to the same image we're seeing here. Same with audio. Nobody can break it. If they try cutting power to the screen, it still turns itself back on."

"How is that possible?" Alvin asked, finally setting the fear to one side for the pure wonder of whatever these Chaa had done, from wherever they were, to do this.

They could have easily blown the station up, if they had that fine of a control over his systems. Just overloaded the reactor and cut the humans out from the control circuits, until the only option left was to order everyone into the emergency escape pods and hope that help could arrive from one of the bases on the lunar surface fast enough to save everyone.

"Unknown, sir," the man answered what should have been obvious as a rhetorical question.

Alvin ignored him. Ignored all of them. Concentrated on the image on the screen.

Okay, mister alien god Chaa, you want us to watch? I'll watch.

Alvin reached down and found that he had the ability to manipulate the camera in three dimensions, zooming and turning. Quickly, he began recognizing faces in the mob.

At least he thought he did. Everyone there looked almost like phantasms rather than corporeal beings. Ghosts you could see through if you squinted just right.

But that was Royston, holding hands with…

What in Creation's name was Fatima Darzi? She had presented herself as a Persian Physicist, the niece of dear, old Firuz Alinejad, one of the great minds of his generation before that tragic accident.

Without that scarf on her head, she had tentacles. And he had touched the woman.

Alvin wondered if he needed something like a tetanus shot now.

But no, if she was an alien spy, she would have done everything in her power not to appear amiss. That would include her health.

It was the others who had suggested killing

everyone on Earth with a bioweapon. That was high on the list of fears that Alvin had assembled with Royston before the man left. If the aliens could open a portal to pull a man like Gareth Dankworth into their universe, they could send a bomb this way.

Or the Black Death.

The other woman with Royston was an Amazon. Alvin was an inch or so taller than Royston, and he would still be looking up to that woman. Elf. Whatever she was.

Her uniform was identical to the one that Gareth was wearing, if that giant creature across the way was the missing man, and not just wearing a close approximation of his face. Except Philippa Loughty seemed to believe it was him.

There were two others as well, one another tall elf and the second a woman who probably out-weighed Alvin, as well as looking down on him.

Attractive too, if you liked Stone Giants.

Another time.

Alvin looked down at the device Royston had left him. The emergency scanner that would sound if it detected a wormhole opening within sixty yards, giving a vector that could be used to direct security teams. Alvin wasn't sure what they might do if it went off.

Still, he was supposed to be in charge. He needed to do something.

"Security, activate all your teams," Alvin said in a firm voice. "Put everyone in life suits for now, prepared to seal up at the slightest warning from their *NBC* scanners."

Nuclear, biological, chemical. All the ways that someone might kill you silently and effectively, without having to blow up your city. Or your base on the dark side of the moon.

"Weapons systems, sir?" the gunner asked, almost excitedly.

"Negative," Alvin replied. "What's coming won't be in a ship, Gunner."

"What will be coming, sir?" someone else asked.

"All of you men are familiar with how Gareth Dankworth disappeared?" Alvin looked around and got back nods and grunts. It was a painful, tragic failure for all of them that the man who might be their greatest agent had just vanished, whereabouts unknown. "Those aliens can open up a wormhole anywhere they want and pluck a man right out of space. Alternatively, they can send through a bomb to destroy us. Or something even worse. There is nothing we can do to stop them, except maintain our duty stations and act like the Earth Force Sky Patrol agents that we are."

On the screen, one of the greater beings suddenly seemed to turn and look right at Alvin. He felt the blood drain out of his soul, leaving everything hollow and cold.

"You are correct, Sector Marshal Alvin Siddall," somebody called *Last Traveler* said simply. "I should have brought you when I brought the others. My apologies, this will not hurt."

And then Alvin found himself standing in the middle of that terrible room. The device in his pocket beeped once and then fell silent. Like he had already traversed a wormhole and landed before either of them realized it.

He looked around in pure awe.

The screen had not done justice to the number of

beings moving like will-o-the-wisps around the ceiling and far walls. Thousands of them, watching, studying, perhaps a few even smiling.

But he was the Sector Marshal of The Arsenal. The second most powerful and important base in Earth Force. He had a responsibility to his people.

Alvin turned in the direction that seemed to be where his invisible camera had last stood.

"Arsenal Forces, this is Sector Marshal Siddall," he said aloud. "I have been transported to wherever it was that the screen shows. Maintain your current duties and let the Commandant know he is now in command of The Arsenal. Otherwise, stand by."

Alvin just hoped that they would hear him. Would understand that there was nothing that they could do but watch. Would continue to act with the highest regard to duty and propriety.

If today was a good day to die, they needed to die well.

Everyone one of them had taken an Oath when they joined Sky Patrol, after all.

Last Traveler was suddenly there. Not confronting him, but well inside his personal space. He felt mental hands somehow rifling through his memory, his very being. It was not painful, but Alvin had the feeling that his entire life was being laid bare before this Chaa, that they could better judge him personally before they executed him.

So be it, he thought at the being. *We have all made mistakes, but there are very few that I regret in a career of service. Do your worst.*

"Oh we will, Alvin Siddall," the being smiled menacingly at him. "We will."

WITNESS

SOMEHOW, Gareth ended up with one arm around Pippa's shoulders, and the other around Talyarkinash as the music played.

He had never been one for the teenage rebellion of rock and roll, but he did understand the power that the band put forth. It was like Talyarkinash had said, the woman up there apparently had the same sorts of psionic potential that he did. That most humans had, perhaps in smaller amounts.

She could embrace an entire auditorium, or whatever this space was, and fill it with her emotions. Make everyone feel them. Live them.

But Gareth was still a human underneath. He hadn't been bound into the *Accord*. Couldn't be, unless one of the Chaa decided to perform the task. He had no doubts they had that sort of power, if they wished.

But with one arm around each woman, he could feel their hearts pounding through their skin. If Pippa's was ever so slighting faster, he could put that down to finally confronting the fact that he wasn't human anymore. That he couldn't marry her and start a family.

Not that it mattered much, if *The Communion* was about to destroy Earth and all the humans anyway.

But so much would be lost.

On the other hand, Gareth understood that the *Accord of Souls* was thousands of times larger than Earth. Trillions of souls would be saved by sacrificing humanity on the altar of the gods.

He just didn't have to like it.

So Gareth listened to the music with his soul, as well as his mind, and let Ellen's words and harmonies fill him with joy. It was like listening to a modern, pop interpretation of Friedrich Schiller's **Ode To Joy**, the anchor movement of Beethoven's Ninth Symphony. Or perhaps **Finlandia**, by Jean Sibelius, dedicated to revolution and resistance against the old Russian Empire.

Perhaps the latter was more appropriate, since rock and roll was always about rebellion.

Both women felt the power flow through them, so maybe human music could speak to an audience of aliens. Not that the *Accord* particularly mattered today, but at least everyone alive today would be able to remember what humanity had once striven for.

Once accomplished.

Gareth looked around and tried to study those beings known as the *Ascended Chaa* for clues. He was a cop. Part of his training had been to sit quietly in a restaurant, surreptitiously studying all the other patrons in the joint, so he could make a guess at their class, education, and how law-abiding they might be when nobody else was around.

Perhaps there had been a touch of magic, of this latent psionic ability, that he could tap. It was all a kind of magic, when you got right down to it.

The *Ascended Chaa* seemed politely inquisitive, at least those he could see, *The Communion* was a wall of blank, white clouds, giving nothing away at all during the performance. The humans and members of the *Accord* around him were as transfixed as he was, raptly absorbed by Ellen's loves, hates, fears, and triumphs.

Perhaps they had all traveled to Hamlin Town.

At one point, Gareth leaned down to kiss Pippa on the head, but she turned up and their lips met instead. It was good. At least they had that before they died.

Gareth had counted twelve songs, hopefully a good number, when the last notes tapered off and the whole world seemed to collapse, like a week-old helium balloon. He sagged with it as the emotions withdrew.

Pippa and Talyarkinash both snuggled closer to him as he held them. Around them, time seemed to start again, but that was just the rush of silence swelling over everything.

Gareth guided the two women over to where his partner and her boss were standing. They seemed to be recovering from the same emotions as everyone else, so hopefully they would have good memories after this as well.

"Pippa, this is Jackeith Grodray and Eveth Baker," Gareth introduced her. "They're with the Constabulary. It's like Earth Force Sky Patrol, but they protect the whole galaxy. I've been working for them. Inspectors Grodray and Baker, Philipa Loughty."

He didn't introduce her as his fiancé. It made no sense at this point, especially as he was only human enough now that he would be destroyed when those gods completed the task they had set out to do.

But the *Accord of Souls* would be safe. He had to keep reminding himself of that. Otherwise, Gareth knew he would fall into such a terrible funk that nothing could ever rescue him.

Not even death.

"Is there anything that can be done?" Pippa asked Eveth after they shook hands.

Baker glanced at him for the briefest moment before she spoke.

"Just before all this happened, Gareth was leading us on an assault that would have either captured or killed Marc Sarzynski," Baker said quietly. "With him gone, there probably would have been no need to do anything so gratuitous. At least one hopes."

"And that is where you are wrong, Inspector," a man's voice intruded.

Gareth spun and saw that Dr. Loughty had stepped close while he wasn't paying attention. Like Gareth, Loughty had two women with him, one a Grace dressed in the uniform of the Earth Force Sky Patrol Women's Auxiliary, which made absolutely no sense.

The other was dressed has he was, in the blue-gray bodysuit of the Constabulary. Unlike the neon-blue badge that Gareth wore, however, hers was brass. That meant that the woman was a Prime

Inspector, like Jackeith and Eveth when they weren't undercover.

Looking at her face, Gareth goggled in shock.

This was Anen Wardson. First Inspector of the Constabulary.

Everyone's boss.

"How so?" Baker asked Dr. Loughty.

"The First Inspector and the *Accord* Commission were in the process of deciding that they should simply go ahead and destroy all of humanity with a bioweapon when *The Communion* intervened," Dr. Loughty said in a firm voice with traces of anger underneath.

"Jackeith Grodray and Eveth Baker, this is Royston Loughty," Gareth introduced the man now. "Pippa's father and one of the most brilliant men in the solar system. One of the greatest men it has ever been my pleasure to know."

They shook hands. Gareth got introduced to the young Grace operative who went by the name of Fatima Darzi. He also met his ultimate boss in the flesh for the first time.

Like Baker, Wardson was Vanir. Perhaps six foot three inches tall, but without the hard athleticism that Baker had, although Gareth could see traces of it in the way she moved.

"This is true?" Grodray asked their boss. "You were about to wipe out the humans?"

"It is," the First Inspector admitted. "Time had grown short, with Sarzynski known to be on Earth, with a working generator station he could use. Predictive modelling suggested that casualties from your assault on Sarzynski's stronghold would be at least seventy percent, so we could not take the chance that you would fail and the man would then be able to recruit an army that he could send back into *Accord* space."

"Then why even bother with the attack?" Baker asked in a voice filled with razor blades.

"You had the Star Dragon with you," the Boss said. "That might have been sufficient to win through. It would have taken my teams at least another hour to prepare the bioweapon, and then we would have begun the targeting process. Had you been successful in bringing me Sarzynski's body, and that of his gang, we could have called things off."

"Except that you would have already made the decision that you could justify wiping humanity out at a later time, correct?" Dr. Loughty asked the woman in a crisp tone.

Gareth felt a small thrill go through him when the First Inspector merely bowed, rather than trying to argue. Loughty was right. It would have been easy from there.

Perhaps the next time there was a hint of criminal activity involving humans. Or the time after that. Pop. Open a portal and throw a vial through it to shatter on the far side and infect anyone within range. Rinse. Repeat.

End of humanity. Perhaps the end of all life on Earth, depending on the nature of the weapon and its ability to quickly mutate across species, like influenza did. Bases like the Arsenal might hold out for a time, but what good would a few thousand men and women on a space station due, if they couldn't grow crops and it wasn't safe to land on any surface?

Another person joined them suddenly, stepping into the small circle of people, even as others stood back and watched in silence. Perhaps those others lived in fear, given the number of humans here and the fact that these people had never encountered such a dangerous creature in the flesh before.

"Excuse me," Petim Diazal said.

Quickly, the small Th'Tarni introduced himself to the folks who had never met him, including Gareth. Except he knew who the man was. Given another year, Petim Diazal would have probably been the one with the final decision on Gareth's fate, one way or the other.

He was nothing like the other Th'Tarni Gareth had met, especially not Gonquah, the fabulously wealthy arms merchant who had manufactured the killer androids for Marc. Gareth could feel the charisma coming off the man like the best cologne, but that was just a measure of what a successful politician would need to be like, at that level of play.

"I wanted to meet the person, the human, about whom so much fear and consternation had centered," Diazal said, bowing slightly to Dr. Loughty as two scholars met in an inn.

"You have the advantage on me, sir," Dr. Loughty replied. "But if I am to understand, you are the head of the *Accord* government?"

"That would be the Proctor, Khozo T'Yuugon," Diazal replied. "An U'Chagi. But circumstances had him on vacation fishing at the moment of our need, so we sent for him, even as we moved forward. I would have probably been the person who signed the declaration, though, yes. My soul would have born the stain when I went to stand before the Creator to explain myself."

Dr. Loughty bowed back and the two studied

each other. The scientist was a little over six feet in height, while the politician was barely Pippa's height in her flats, but both men were mental titans that put the rest of the audience to shame.

"So where does that leave us?" Dr. Loughty asked the group in a simple voice. "We have heard the music of our illustrious songstress. We have gathered into a conclave that I hope will not devolve into a battlefield. All voices are hopefully present. What is next?"

"Now the Judgment will begin," *Speaker for the Communion* announced in a voice that echoed across a thousand worlds, and every place in the Solar System where humans existed to hear it.

DEFENDER

ROYSTON HAD the feeling that those twelve Gods, the beings of *The Communion*, had almost been waiting for someone to speak. To spark the inevitable. It had been his bad luck, perhaps, to draw that straw, but someone would have done it eventually.

He turned in the direction of the dais upon which the Chaa gods had assembled. Studied their glyphs again, since each seemed to be an identical cloud of light up there to the eyes.

First Immortal. Great Teacher. Seeker for the Knee of God. Uplifter. Glory in Sunrise. Merciless. Speaker For The Communion. Narrator of History. Mountain. Astray in Darkness. Magistrate. Last Traveler.

All of them represented so much power that Royston couldn't even begin to calculate it. Collectively, he had no idea if they had any limits, save their imaginations. With the lesser beings, the *Ascended Chaa*, present he wondered what it might be that they could not do.

Merciless had already made it known that he had once destroyed an entire species of star-traveling explorers. Brigands, granted, but probably no worse than humans might have been on a bad day. And that was merely one of them. He could call on the assistance of his peers, but that would be unnecessary.

Just dropping a singularity into *Earth*'s Solar System, close enough to disrupt the sun, would be sufficient to end humanity. It wasn't like they had ever sent generational colony ships to places like *Centauri* in order to expand humanity's footprint.

And until Royston Loughty had found the door, humans had been trapped in their home system forever.

"This Court is in session," *Speaker for the Communion* announced with a tone that implied a gavel striking the bench. "Much is already known, but there is much yet to understand. *Last Traveler*, you have called us thus, for reasons all too obvious, but the bulk of humanity cannot achieve glyphs, so their ignorance remains in place. Speak to this assembled body the basic facts. I would have humanity *understand* their crimes."

Royston watched the being move from his place at one end of the platform to stand down with the lesser beings, like a prosecuting attorney smiling grimly at the audience and the jury as he prepared his case. Royston almost expected him to put his thumbs into non-existent suspenders and grin as he turned to the rest of the room.

"Seven Chitra ago, the Chaa gathered together and planned that creation that would become the *Accord of Souls*," *Last Traveler* spoke with a florid, circular tone that seemed to emerge from all corners of the room simultaneously. "Roughly Seventy-two thousand human years, as such things are measured. Several worlds were known to have life upon them, but none other than *Almar* had advanced as far as even metals technology. Thus were the Chaa the first of the Creator's Children to be able to go seek Him."

Royston nodded, listening as the being glyphed his words as well as spoke them in what he heard as standard Queen's English. Gareth would probably hear a distinct, Indiana twang in his own head.

"The first Great Debate was whether or not humanity should be included in the roster of new species that would be uplifted to join the *Accord*," Last Traveler continued. "Unlike most of the other species, humans were already significantly advanced, with stone tools and cave art showing off a sophistication well in advance of any of the others we considered. The others were still yet perhaps highly intelligent animals by comparison, lacking language and tool use."

He turned and smiled at Royston, as if acknowledging the Defense Counsel who would become his principle opponent.

"At the same time, humans are an exceedingly violent species in their native form," the Chaa said in a darker tone. "They make war on one another for the thinnest of reasons and often no good excuse at all, save that *other* might be a different skin tone or speak the same language with a different accent."

Royston nodded back, all too aware of the history of his species when it came to violence. If anything, things had gotten so much worse, with the advent of ever-more-sophisticated technology, that humans should have probably never emerged from the Twentieth or Twenty-First Centuries, but rather destroyed themselves then.

When no guilt would fall on anybody but humans for the outcome.

"You would challenge my conclusions?" *Last Traveler* suddenly focused his attention on Royston, as if detecting a note of dismay.

"Not in whole," Royston countered him deftly. "But I would offer that humans do recognize such tendencies, and have, at least in modern times, worked to reduce such violence to manageable levels, as we try to become something better. Earth Force, and more particularly Sky Patrol, are dedicated arms of the World Government that exist to end wars, sir. Crime is a different matter, and there our efforts have not been as successful."

"Let it be noted," *Last Traveler* pulled a glyph directly out of Royston's mind as he watched, and then transmitted it to the others.

All the others: human, alien, and Chaa alike.

The founding of Earth Force in the late Twenty-First Century as a quasi-military arm of the World Governing Council and the Hall of Governments, before it simply became the government itself, while allowing all the nations to retain local control.

The advent of Sky Patrol, when it became understood that wars might have ended, but that humanity needed a single law enforcement agency tasked with protecting the entire Solar System, regardless of lesser jurisdiction.

Royston felt a smile as *Last Traveler* reached into the mind of Alvin Siddall and pulled forth some of that man's memories. Hopefully, the Chaa understood that some of the things in Royston's mind should be taken to his grave as secrets, rather than shared in open court.

Royston had been a Sky Patrol agent in his youth, although he never talked about it. Could never talk about it, without being brought up on charges for violating a number of Official Secrets Act sections. As he had said, war on an industrial scale might be gone, but there were still men and women born whose megalomania would not let them settle for anything less than domination of all things.

Some of those psychopaths turned to politics, where their faulty emotional wiring probably served them well.

But others…

Yes. Best not to discuss men like Gergely Cseh. Better still if everyone forgot the man ever existed, lest someone decide to emulate him and try to take over the entire world with blackmail and mad science.

He had been another one like Gareth or Ellen, possessed of an oversized psionic ability he could tap. And a heart as black a night.

Last Traveler had obviously seen those memories, and left them be. That was for everyone's benefit tonight.

Instead, they watched Alvin's memories play out. A much younger man, back when he was another one like Gareth, tall and muscular, and intent on making everything better. A successful career climbing the ladder, from 0-1 Deputy Agent all the way up to 0-7 and Sector Marshal, second only to the Sky Marshal himself, the Head of Sky Patrol.

Alvin's life had been much more public than Royston's, just another beat cop turned detective.

"I would pause now to prepare everyone." *Last Traveler* said quietly. "The memories I have shown until now have been Alvin Siddall, Sector Marshal of Sky Patrol and one of their top commanders; and Royston Loughty, PhD, WMU, FRS, CBE, CStJ. We have seen how Earth Force came about, and why it was necessary. We have witnessed the purpose and execution of Sky Patrol. All of these are simple things. Straight forward and public knowledge. Now we must turn to the present tense."

Royston watched the godlike being turn to face a corner of the room that everyone else had mostly ignored, partly out of necessity, partly out of spite. The spot where an invisible demarcation separated Marc Sarzynski and his gang from the rest, like an old-fashioned, three-strand electric fence holding in restive cattle, back home in Montana.

Royston got the impression of a hand waved across the room, much like the ancient wizards might have done on a vid for visual effect.

He watched Marc being bodily lifted into the air, hovering futilely as *Last Traveler* carried him to the center of the room, not all that far from where Royston and Gareth stood. At the same time, Royston felt a second force wrap psychic tentacles around his body, preventing him from simply grabbing Sarzynski by the neck and strangling that son of a bitch to death.

No doubt Gareth felt the same force. Glancing around, most of the people within close proximity were under the same compulsion. It was good to know that hatred of evil spanned cultures and species.

"Marc Sarzynski, also known publicly as the criminal Maximus, you are summoned," *Last Traveler* said unnecessarily, although people watching at home might not grasp the finer points of today's charade.

"We have seen the recent history of Earth Force and Sky Patrol," the Chaa prosecutor said in a harder voice than Royston had heard before. "It is my understanding that Marc Sarzynski once swore those same oaths as the Sky Patrol agents in this room."

Again, Royston caught what looked like a wicked gleam in the eye of *Last Traveler*, glancing his way and nodding at their shared secret. Not even Pippa knew, because Royston had retired from active duty and taken up science as a vocation when he married dear Elizabeth, God rest her soul.

"Now we will see how a dedicated, honored Sky Patrol agent turned to evil," *Last Traveler*'s voice oozed a vicious ichor now.

Royston knew most of the story. Had witnessed it firsthand as the boys became men and the men moved from friendly rivals to deadly enemies. All over a woman. A very special woman, to be noted.

Pippa.

But then, the Trojan War had, at the end of the day, been driven by two men's love for the same woman.

Royston had read a number of translations of The Iliad over the decades. They all began with some variation of that most human, most powerful of emotions.

Sing for me, oh Muse, a song of the Rage of Achilles.

But everyone left out the other, greater battle: Menelaus and Paris. They spoke of the honorable warrior wronged and doomed to live and die such a short, powerful life, but left out two men's war over one woman, and the tremendous socio-political earthquake that resulted in the sacking of Troy, the wanderings of Odysseus, and the betrayal of Agamemnon.

Today was different, though. Last Traveler picked Marc's memories and turned them into emotional glyphs that others could absorb without words.

Two young men, as close to perfection as humanly possible perhaps, thrown together as freshmen roommates. Competitions in the classroom, on the track, and on the field. Friendly, for the most part.

Two men, never separated by more than a few hundredths of a point in academia, or as much as a tenth of a second in athletics.

Royston knew, from old records he had perused in his investigations of the man, that Elders of both Sky Patrol and Earth Force eventually expected that Marc Sarzynski had a significant chance to become Sky Marshal. To become the commander of the entire Sky Patrol.

That was the one place the two men differed temperamentally. Gareth would have had to have been blackmailed by his superiors to accept a promotion above Senior Special Agent, knowing that to become a Commandant, a base commander somewhere, would make the end of his days as a field agent.

But alas, it was not to be.

Instead, Royston watched as both men became

Deputy Agents and first encountered him, and more importantly, Pippa.

If the rivalry at school had been nearly off the charts, the competition to catch his daughter's eye went an order of magnitude beyond that. Always friendly, but never-ending in the game.

And it had been so pointless, at the end. Marc Sarzynski had never lacked for available female companionship, as Royston knew. But Pippa had chosen Gareth, the simpler boy from Indiana over the one from New Metropolis.

Marc Sarzynski never got over losing that competition.

Royston understood better than the rest watching today, what had happened next. The subtle changes that came over the man, only evident in retrospect. The darkness that took root. The never-displayed rage that displaced the grief and depression Marc Sarzynski would never allow to take root.

The understanding that the Solar System really wasn't big enough for the two of them, like two old-time gunfighters facing off at high noon on a dirt street in front of a saloon. It had never happened that way, although the galaxy might be better off if it had.

Instead, Marc simply resigned his commission and walked away from Sky Patrol, in spite of all the conversations with superiors and attempted inducements to get him to stay.

Again, how might the world have turned out, the entire galaxy, had Marc been able to heal his broken heart and perhaps settle for the second greatest woman alive? Any number of them would have been happy to become Mrs. Sarzynski. Of that, Royston had no doubts whatsoever.

What would have happened to the *Accord of Souls* with another man? The crime lord known as Cinnra, a birdman creature known as Warreth, had asked his scientists to locate him a human killer, an assassin that he could use as a sharp instrument, in a galaxy that did not understand violence and could not apparently practice it upon one another.

The two Yuudixtl, Xiomber and Morty, had obliged the being, and found him the single most dangerous man alive in the Solar System. What would have happened had they just picked a common thug, like the one human who had been standing with Marc.

Royston didn't know who Two-Gun Kowalski was, but he read the man's glyph now, and saw a remorseless, merciless killer, but not one with the possibilities of Marc Sarzynski. No, that would have been satisfied with a galaxy of people he could kill, and not demanded more.

Not overthrown Cinnra and taken over his gang, as Marc apparently had. Did, as Royston watched *Last Traveler* pull those memories from Marc's mind and display his crimes to the whole galaxy.

Royston had a strong stomach. He had needed it in the old days, to do some of the things he had. He needed it now, watching Marc bring his brilliance and powerful drive to the task of purging Cinnra's gang of anyone who would not bow his head fast enough. The killings that cleared out any suspected of disloyalty. Rebuilding the gang with only the most ruthless men and women he could find and still trust.

Of surviving when he had been cast into an alien landscape where every hand was turned against him.

Royston watched the man's criminal genius

blossom. He studied Maiair and Yooyar as Marc saw them: assistants, accomplices, and lovers. Like one of the ancient newsreels, the story unfolded, showing crimes and corruptions so brazen and expansive that Royston was amazed that anybody had been able to stop Marc, let alone topple him.

Last Traveler paused here, the waves of rage pulsing off the being even greater than that of the other eleven, if such a thin margin could be measured.

"That's only half the story, bub," a voice rang out, just as angry, if only smaller because the man projecting it wasn't a god. "Tell the other half before you completely poison the jury and I move for a mistrial."

Royston expected the Yuudixtl, Morty if he was correct in trying to tell them apart physically, would be snuffed from existence by one of The Communion for such effrontery, but instead the words drew a chuckle from one of the other Chaa.

"I doubt that you would be able to file a successful motion for a change of venue," *Narrator of History* seemed almost mirthful. "We have not located the Creator Who Bore Us yet and no others have advanced enough to be our peers, in any of the galaxies or planes of existence we have sought Him."

"Fine," Morty snapped grumpily. "It is my turn now?"

Royston found himself liking the little lizardman, as he read the complicated glyphs the Yuudixtl scientist projected, and saw how the others, the ones he thought of as the good guys, reacted to the man.

"Indeed," *Last Traveler* said. "Perhaps it is time to

hear from the one most responsible for the greatest crime in the last five Chitra."

"And your salvation, princess," Morty snarked back hard. "Don't forget that part."

Rather than answer, *Last Traveler* picked up Morty in a field similar to Marc and held him aloft. A moment later, Morty's egg-brother Xiomber joined him.

Egg-brother? What an interesting concept. Royston looked forward to the little man's story.

He would need something useful, when he pled with the gods to do something less than simply wiping out all of humanity.

EGG BROTHER

SOMEHOW, Morty had always known it was going to end up like this. As he and Xiomber had always teased each other: how bad could it be if the Chaa didn't show up to stop us?

Until they did. You roll the dice enough times, and eventually the worst possible result will come up.

Statistical certainty.

"So, yeah, I own that," Morty said to the executioners up on their platform. "Cinnra wanted a killer, so I went and found him the best, meanest one I could. Not my fault that nobody would listen then I told them that they couldn't control a monster like that. Even Xiomber thought I was loony."

"Loonier than usual," his egg-brother replied, just before he squawked when the Chaa dude picked him up and added him to the shooting gallery. "What?"

"You hadda open yer mouth, egg-brother," Morty laughed. "Gonna get you in trouble, one of these days."

"You mean like facing a death sentence from a dozen angry gods with an axe to grind?" Xiomber snapped at him.

"Worse," Morty laughed. "I'll tell Mom on you."

You weren't supposed to laugh at gods. Stuff like that irritated the hell out of them, at least in the books. But that got a good chuckle from everyone, so Morty counted it as a win when nobody gacked him for it.

"Yes, I was the one that programmed the machine to locate Maximus," Morty said. "Already admitted to it in an *Accord* Court of Justice and just awaiting my final sentencing for treason, okay? But that's only the first half of the story."

He took a deep breath and wondered if he would land on his feet, if the Chaa dropped him from five meters in the air. He wasn't a Nari, or someone graceful like that. Probably faceplant pretty hard.

But how bad could it be if the Chaa didn't show up to stop you?

Indeed.

"Then one morning, I woke up in a cold sweat," Morty continued, feeling his voice dial itself down from sarcastic clown to serious scientist.

He hated when that happened, but really didn't have any control over it. Cost of doing business, when you worked for criminals who usually didn't have a sense of humor.

"It was a simple issue, really," Morty continued. "What the hell had I done?"

The room didn't laugh this time, but he hadn't expected them to. Shit had just gotten serious. Angry gods with itchy trigger fingers, and all that.

"I hadda ask myself a simple question: Could

anything stop Maximus, once he decided he was going to just take over the entire *Accord of Souls* as Emperor Marc the First?" Morty asked the rest of them.

Interestingly, it was the cops that seemed to understand him and offer some level of support, from the looks on their faces. Even Liamssen smiled at him, and she had the most reason to hate him and his egg-brother, at least at first.

Gods alone knew what had changed after the raid that separated them. He and Xiomber had been too busy running for their lives.

"Like I told my egg-brother, if you've just burned your house down, you don't get to complain when you have to sleep in the backyard in the mud, while it rains," Morty's voice took on an even-more-sober tone now.

He could feel somebody rooting around in his head, but ignored it as much as he could. It almost felt like an itch under that one scale you can't reach, no matter how you twist. When you have to either find a good post to scratch against, or have an egg-brother who'll help.

Images ghosted the room as he watched, as he spoke, so Morty figured that he was just providing a running, color commentary as the Chaa broadcast all his secrets to the universe.

Of course, by now, every cop in the *Accord* had probably read his and Xiomber's initial statements, rather than the cut-down versions leaving out all the jay walking, parking tickets, and overdue library fines, so it wasn't like he had many things left to conceal.

"So now I had to do something about it," Morty

explained matter-of-factly. "I had to undo the evil that I had caused to come into being. It was impossible at that point to just grab Maximus and send him home, because we had had to turn him from a human into a Vanir, at least physically, in order to hide in the *Accord*. Plus, any portal we tried to draw him through he would have avoided easy enough, and then come for us with guns blazing."

Morty had just enough freedom of movement to look over at his old boss and sneer at the man.

"Ya scare people too much, and they do stupid things, Maximus," Morty told the man, hopefully safe from the giant reaching over and crushing his skull with one of those giant paws.

But nothing happened, other than a flair of pure hatred in the man's eyes.

Betrayal, perhaps, but hey, you brought it on yourself, bucko.

Deep breath. You've already admitted it. Own it.

"So now I had to find something to stop the most dangerous monster in the *Accord of Souls*," Morty said, looking around until he found the one person he wanted to talk to now. "And I couldn't even tell my egg-brother, at least not until right at the end, for fear he'd decide he was more afraid of Maximus's reach than his rage. I went looking for a hero."

HERO

GARETH BLUSHED to hear the words from Morty.

He had never set out to be a hero. All he ever wanted was to do right and see good things happen in the world. So he supposed that maybe that made him a hero, at least when circumstances conspired to demand it of him.

How many other people took a step back, at that moment, instead of a step forward?

But he had taken an Oath. Earth Force Sky Patrol. Heroes, if you will. Stepping up to confront injustice and criminality, in whatever form it took.

"Since I had programmed the machine to find Maximus, from among all humans, it was easy enough to pretty much reverse everything when looking for someone to become his Nemesis," Morty continued, eyes locked with Gareth's now, as a strange river of energy seemed to connect them.

Fate?

"At the time, I had no idea just how exactly I had managed my settings," Morty said. "A human who was psychologically the exact opposite of Maximus in every way, but still his physical and mental equal. I would need that, in order to fight the ultimate crime boss and save the *Accord of Souls* from being conquered by that human."

Gareth nodded. He had watched the images drawn from Marc's memory. From his very soul. Seen the man, who once might have been his best man, turn into his worst nightmare: a rogue cop.

Everything they had been taught, Marc perverted, because he understood both sides of the law better than anyone alive. And yet, it hadn't been enough, in the face of the might of Earth Force Sky Patrol. Gareth had come within eight minutes of capturing Marc at the same time as he caught the rest of the gang.

Although, in retrospect, Morty might have simply pulled him out of the back of a Black Maria van. Assuming, of course, that Marc Sarzynski was somehow taken alive.

What would those eight minutes have meant to humanity, had Marc died during that shootout?

Morty would have taken someone else, but whoever he had gone after in the absence of Marc Sarzynski would have been Junior Varsity by comparison. Maybe enough to do the job for Cinnra, but nothing that was a threat to the rest of the galaxy.

But then, would the *Accord of Souls* have simply collapsed, like the Roman Empire had, when people forgot to work every day at upholding their legacy? Maybe it would have taken another century, from what Gareth's studies had shown, but the structure was rotting and close to collapse when Marc arrived.

He had only hastened the final fall.

At least, until Morty had needed a hero.

"You roll the dice enough times, and bad things happen," Morty said. "But good things do, too. Xiomber decided to help me instead of shooting me, at the end. Him telling the rest of the gang wouldn't have stopped me, because I had my getaway planned and it worked. We were all gone to *Orgoth Vortai* with Gareth in tow before anybody could stop us. Scared the hell out that poor girl in the tea shop. Discovered that no woman can apparently resist the man's animal magnetism, species be damned. Fled again, until we found Talyarkinash and challenged her to outdo everything she had ever even dreamed of. I'm just sorry my and Xiomber weren't there at the end to see how it all worked, having run like hell when Baker and Grodray showed up."

Gareth felt the attention of the Chaa known as *Last Traveler* as it turned and located Talyarkinash, still snuggled up to his side opposite Pippa. It was like a searchlight seeking bombers overhead on a cold, dark night.

She stiffened and tried to grasp Gareth's side, but the Chaa pulled her away and into the air, just as he had the other three.

Gareth's motion to prevent the man never even made it to his nerves, so *Last Traveler* must have simply blocked him from moving, like he had stopped Gareth from killing Marc earlier.

Was there nothing he could do to protect his friends from these gods?

GENETICIST

TALYARKINASH WANTED TO SCREAM.

Would have, if the monster holding her aloft would have allowed it. It was almost rape, the way he simply overrode all of her motor control and turned her into a puppet, dangling in the air at his mercy and whim.

To take, without ever asking.

She wanted to rage. To tear his throat out with her teeth and hands, if she could just move. And if the creature had a physical body she could kill.

"Your hands are not clean," *Last Traveler* strobed his anger at her before relenting. "But neither are they entirely dirty. You will speak, or I will compel it."

Rape. That's what you're talking about, you son of a bitch. Do what I want and I won't hurt you.

If she could have only spoken those words aloud. But she saw something in his eyes (?) at that moment. Some understanding that he had let his gender do things to her that were not acceptable.

A tiny apology passed, and Talyarkinash found herself standing on the ground, instead of hanging in the air for a god's entertainment like the three men. Her feet would not take a step, but her hands were free.

The agony in Gareth's eyes turned to rage as she watched. Talyarkinash realized that his first instinct had been to step forward, to shield her from the anger of a Chaa. To even challenge the being and fight him. If that was even possible.

But this was Gareth. He would absolutely try.

Amazingly, Pippa and the Grace woman, Fatima, were both allowed to approach her. Perhaps they were also compelled, but it looked like a word of encouragement from *Last Traveler*, rather than taking possession of their bodies and forcing them to do his will.

Each stood close and simply took one her hands in both of theirs. Talyarkinash could feel the support, the love, flow from both women, to prop her up in those places where everything wanted to simply curl up in a ball and whimper.

Or leap at a god and rend him.

She still wasn't sure which emotion would win.

Talyarkinash took a breath and held it as long as she could, trying to find the center of her being.

Something from Pippa held her upright. But Talyarkinash knew Gareth as well. She would understand that man's instincts to protect. To fight, even against impossible odds.

To walk first into a wormhole, attacking Sarzynski's stronghold, knowing that there was a high likelihood he would be the first to die. Because that might open the way for Baker and Grodray to do something afterwards.

Yes, that was Gareth. And Pippa as well, as she studied the woman she had long since stopped thinking of as a rival. Philippa Loughty had no rivals for Gareth's love. That much had become evident quickly, and nothing Talyarkinash had seen had changed her opinion of the man.

Instead, she turned to the Chaa and let her anger show. There was nothing a Nari geneticist could do that would even get the attention of a god, and they both knew it, but the monster had the courtesy to look chagrined.

"Morty and Xiomber brought Gareth to me on *Hurquar*," Talyarkinash finally said when she felt like she could talk rationally. "I will never forget that day, because Gareth made such an unbelievable impression on me. I have not been able to isolate it to a pheromone or anything like that, but he had that effect on most of the women he had encountered, regardless of species."

She took another breath and let the storytelling wash some of the rage out of her soul. Thinking about Gareth calmed her. Explaining what Morty's idea of *Hero* meant for the rest of the *Accord* was something that would keep her from wanting to kill a god for his arrogance.

"There is another Nari woman named Alicia, somewhere in Hurquar," Talyarkinash continued. "I heard the story from Xiomber later, about how she just happened to be behind them on the slidewalk and gave Gareth her scent card, with her contact information in vermillion ink."

She chuckled at the thought, mostly to herself, before looking back up and fixing her stare on *Last Traveler*.

"Had she known he was human, I doubt she would have behaved any differently," Talyarkinash growled at the god. "It is a measure of his charisma, his power. Something I later assumed was a factor of that same, immense psionic ability that allowed the Star Dragon. He has no comprehension about what he does to women, so his innocence is all the more endearing, but he walked into my lab and Morty and Xiomber needed a favor."

Deep breath to control her other emotions, before she showed everyone in the room, perhaps in the galaxy, how much she had been in love with the man from that moment. She could never tell him, he wouldn't have seen her. But he had been an even better friend than he ever would have been a lover. Had made her feel safe, even when they were on the run from Maximus. Had traded that criminal's freedom for her life, when he could have easily destroyed them both, that first night when the Star Dragon first appeared.

Flames, claws, or teeth, there was nothing Marc Sarzynski could have done to stop Gareth's rage. And Gareth had let him walk away, simply to protect her. Had risked the entire galaxy, to protect one Nari criminal.

Talyarkinash glanced at the man who had started it all. Another human like Gareth, but darker. Angrier. Another one she felt so deeply for that she sometimes didn't know herself.

But she could see the faint echoes of the man who

had been Gareth's best friend a decade ago. Not all traces of that other man, another cop who had wanted to make the world better, were gone. Buried, perhaps, behind the rage and the will to power, but even then limiting things.

Punishing him with pain and regret, even as the criminal overlord found it necessary to torture another soul and kill him. It had brought him no joy. It brought him no solace now.

Just things that had to be done.

Talyarkinash had not understood that before. She had had to know Gareth to understand that supremely human thing: to walk into the fire, at whatever personal cost, because that was the duty cast upon you.

"I was utterly opposed, until Morty and Xiomber explained to me what they were really about," she continued her narrative. "How Maximus was going to take over the entire galaxy if somebody didn't do something to stop him. How they had gone back to the well for another human, this one a cop who might be able to stop Maximus from destroying the very *Accord of Souls.*"

She wanted to reach out and just touch Gareth on the arm now. Remind him of the good things that he had accomplished, because she could see the memories of that day taking center stage in his mind. The rage. The sadness. The commitment.

"There was one thing that the boys hadn't told Gareth," she said in a quieter voice, reliving it herself as she waited for a renegade human to go berserk and kill them all. "He was here to stop Maximus, but afterwards, it would never be possible for him to go home. No knowledge of the *Accord of Souls* was allowed on Earth, lest the humans realize that they really weren't alone and figured out how to escape and do something about it."

Gareth's eyes fell. She traced and realized that wistful sign was aimed at Pippa, standing close. As it should be.

"I watched Gareth commit to giving up everything in order to stop Marc Sarzynski's conquest," she turned back to the first god, and then the rest. "Everything. Earth Force Sky Patrol. His friends. *Pippa*. Because he would never be allowed to return. And that only caused him to pause for the briefest moment."

Talyarkinash reached deep into her memory and pushed that memory out to where the rest of the galaxy might understand.

Gareth, standing in her lab, having just learned the truth from her, without the careful, mental preparation that Morty and Xiomber had planned, to bring him along slowly.

Yes, the rage. The sadness. The commitment.

"Gareth's words: *He's here, and he must be stopped. Whatever the cost.*" Talyarkinash fixed her eyes on *Last Traveler*. "Do you understand what that means? What he sacrificed? Everything. And it was a price he was willing to pay. Can any of you say the same?"

She felt the being take a metaphorical step back, although none of them moved and Talyarkinash doubted that anyone else witnessed it. But she did. And that was enough.

"Tell me about the transformation," the Chaa ordered in a soft, polite tone. Finally asking instead of compelling.

"First, you need to understand Marc Sarzynski," she replied, casting her voice out to all the hosts of heaven and hell gathered around her. "He was human, like Gareth. Six feet, two inches tall. Roughly two hundred and forty-five pounds of Earth Force Sky Patrol Agent. Among the very best. Both of them."

Again, she glanced over at the dark man and read his soul, somehow exposed by the gods for everyone to do the same. So much like Gareth, and yet so different.

"They didn't tell me what Sarzynski was when they brought him to me, Morty and Xiomber." She picked up the thread and concentrated. "He was just a non-*Accord* alien they wanted turned into a Vanir. I am a geneticist. One of the very best in the business. My professional pride saw it as a challenge. I was able to turn him into the being you see now. Seven feet, four inches tall. Three hundred and forty pounds. Bigger, faster, and stronger than any of the Vanir I know. Morty and Xiomber tell me that after I was done they then turned Marc into a genius as well, functionally doubling his mental capacity to make him among the greatest warlords in history. Even human history."

Talyarkinash could not suppress the shudder that passed through her soul, thinking about what an Empire under Marc Sarzynski would have been like.

The non-gods around her gasped as well, whether it was because they saw what she saw, or merely understood the dreadful implications.

Talyarkinash wondered how close to immortality a human could get with the right geneticist challenging Time itself.

"So when they brought me a second human, and told me what he really was and why he was in my lab, I had an even greater challenge ahead of me," she smiled in spite of her emotional turmoil. "Especially when Gareth explained how he thought he could win."

STAR DRAGON

GARETH LISTENED to Talyarkinash's words and tried to keep himself composed. Centered.

Calm.

He represented all humans today, including all the billions who would never understand what was going on.

Last Traveler turned to him now. Faced Gareth from across the space. Gareth kept the growl inside when it really wanted to escape and paint itself all over a lesser god, however powerful the being might be.

"Star Dragon," the Chaa said.

Gareth couldn't tell if it was a question, a form of address, or something else. Gareth just nodded back at him.

"Star Dragon," he agreed.

"Why?" the creature asked.

Suddenly, all twelve of *The Communion* were focused on him. And thousands of their kin. And billions of humans.

And all of the *Accord of Souls*, however many trillions of people that was. And they were people, each and every one.

He didn't care what shape they took. What planet they were born. What gods they might worship.

They were his friends. His comrades.

The souls he had sworn to protect, first when he became a Deputy Agent of Earth Force Sky Patrol, even if he didn't know it at the time. Or later, when Grodray and Baker allowed him to take on the blue-gray body suit, and the neon-blue badge of the Constabulary.

To protect the innocent from harm.

"I have always been an even match for Marc Sarzynski," Gareth explained slowly, breathing the words in and out as he delved back into his memories. "In track and field, we swapped first and second place on a daily basis, even event by event. In academics, even a razor's edge was too thin to separate us. We are the same person, he and I."

And they were. The other gods, those watching over humans when the Chaa weren't around, could be credibly accused of playing a dark practical joke on humanity, to send two men to school together at the same time, and make them so alike in every way.

"Or were," Gareth continued. "Until we met Pippa and both fell madly in love with her."

He turned to look at the woman, ignoring the rest of eternity for a moment.

"She could only pick one, and for the longest time, neither of us knew which it would be," Gareth sighed, both with joy and sadness. "That was the greatest day of my life, when she chose me. None of us understood what that would mean, though."

He pushed his own memories up and out, letting one of the being project it to the rest of the galaxy.

Nobody had understood what an inflection point had been passed, until much later. Marc didn't stop caring, but stopped caring as much. Found other things to focus on, but he had been infected with darkness.

Eventually, it took him fully, and the man walked away from his career as a crime-fighter, seeking another path. The darker one.

Destroyer, as it were.

The pursuit then, as Agents of Sky Patrol, often led by Gareth himself, chased the man through the underworld and darkness, never quite catching him.

Eventually, the UnderHives of Mars, where they had finally treed the fox and were circling for the capture when the man disappeared from sight. The rest of the gang had gone down with no understanding of how their boss had vanished.

Eventually, the best theory that remained, when the rest were discarded, suggested that Marc had somehow hypnotized his men to remember a flash of golden light and nothing else. One boss escaping and leaving his men alone for the cops.

Some rolled at that point, there being no honor among thieves, at least the angry kind. Marc's network was unraveled, dismantled. Eliminated.

And yet, nobody knew what happened to Marc Sarzynski.

Gone, without a trace.

Earth Force and Sky Patrol sought, but could find nothing that led them to how Marc had escaped, or where he might be hiding.

Gone, without any trace.

Gareth turned to study the man who was so much him that it was almost painful, some days.

Vanir, yes. Both of them, now, but he was still recognizable underneath, with the same jaw, the same hair, the same shoulders. Bigger eyes. Almost-ridiculous ears, at least to human sensibilities. Monsters compared to the humans around them that he had known and loved for so long.

"We are the same person," Gareth mused again. "When they made him better, they did the same to me, but that just meant we both started over with a clean slate, and a thousand times larger sandbox in which to pursue one another. And I would be just as much a hunted criminal as Marc, because I was a human, loose in the *Accord of Souls*, regardless of what Talyarkinash did to change me or what my mission was to save everyone else. I needed something more. An edge. A symbol, both of hope to the innocent, and fear to the criminal."

Gareth drew a deep breath and thought back to his youth. The comic books his parents let him collect, filled with stories both ancient and modern. *The Iliad* and the *Odyssey. Beowulf.* St. George and the Dragon. There and Back Again. Stories where a dragon was a monster to be feared and fought by the heroes.

But also King Arthur and his Knights. Arthur *Pendragon.* Heroes under a dragon's pennon. Protectors.

At first, he had been unsure if such a symbol would inspire as much awe and fear from the peoples of the *Accord* as it would humans, but then Morty had explained his psionic ability to Gareth in a way even a cop could understand. At least well enough.

He couldn't actually fly with those wings. His body would be too heavy, unless those wings were ten times as far across and he was built more like a Chinese dragon, a *Lung*, than the more European version he had in mind.

But it didn't involve physics, what he did. It was basically just *magic*.

There were other terms for it, but none of them were any more exact or illuminating than anything else.

Magic.

But if magic could make him over into a terrible, fire-breathing, flying lizard, what couldn't it do? Could it inspire the legendary dragonfear that had been at the heart of so many fables?

Only one way to find out.

Except that Marc had found them at the worst possible instant.

Kicked in the door while Gareth was woozy from the drugs and the transform viruses inside his system, *altering* him.

Marc walked in and stunned him unconscious. Helpless.

Failure.

Captured Talyarkinash, as well. Somehow Marc was able to ambush Grodray and Baker in the ensuing mess, taking everyone who might have been able to stop him.

Gareth felt the attention of *Last Traveler* waver at that moment. Like a light went out as the being turned his attention elsewhere.

To Gareth, his muscles sagged, and he suddenly

realized how tense he had been, pushing back against the Chaa, even with his mind, if not his body.

"Prime Investigator Jackeith Grodray, I would have your story," the Chaa announced.

Grodray surprised Gareth by just smiling and the being and shaking his head.

"Not my story," Grodray said. "I was just a watcher. This is Eve's tale to tell."

Last Traveler turned to the other Constable. The other Prime Investigator.

Gareth could tell how much more careful the being had learned to be, when approaching a female with his powers and deciding to *compel* them to do something.

Gareth wasn't the only one in this room who had taken offense.

"Eveth Baker, I would have your story, then," the Chaa called out more politely than he had.

Baker scowled that magnificent way she did and stepped up. Gareth watched her take a breath and sneer at the assembled gods as she focused her attention.

Gareth smiled.

PRIME INVESTIGATOR

"WE HAD BEEN SEEKING rumors of a human loose in the *Accord*," Eveth growled at the man, the creature. The apparent Chaa of *The Communion* known as *Last Traveler*. Whatever that kind of a name really meant. "This was before Gareth, back when Cinnra first captured Sarzynski."

Had it really been less than two years ago when all this started? Eveth had a hard time framing everything into such a small window of time, such a small box.

And yet, that was the truth.

"As a young, hotshot Constable on *Orgoth Vortai*, I had been assigned to be the junior partner to a Senior Constable more or less brought in to watch me and see where my career was going," she continued, turning to Jack with a smile. "He might not have ever said that out loud, but I knew how to put disparate pieces together. They wanted to know if I was good enough to handle the job."

Eveth let her mind drift back. At the edges of her consciousness, she felt fingers tapping on the window pane of her soul, rather than just grabbing hold and squeezing her for information, like the being had done to Talyarkinash.

She had wondered if the Nari woman would jump the son of a bitch and rip his throat out over that. Eveth had almost done it for her, until *Last Traveler* recognized his mistake.

Power does not automatically make you right.

Eveth let the god have her memories to share.

"And then a rumor of a second human loose reached us," she continued. "We all had roles to play, and I played mine well. Bad cop, as it were, relying on intuition, while the cerebral Jack Grodray was the intellectual detective. We were chasing our second supposed rogue human."

She glanced at the *rogue human*. Laughed to herself at how far they had all come together in such a short period of time. That *rogue human* was possibly the best partner she had ever had, excepting only Jack.

"At the time, nobody understood just how deep so many planetary governments had fallen into corruption," Eveth snarled at the universe. "Petty things, but they add up, like water slowly carving a canyon through the mountains. *Orgoth Vortai* wasn't as bent as *Hurquar*, but we were on the trail and dared not tell anyone. At least until we had better evidence to take to Jack's superiors. This was when I still though he was just a Level-4, a mere Senior Constable forced to partner with a hothead to tone her down some."

That got a smile from Jack.

"Didn't work," he murmured just loud enough that several of the people nearby chuckled in response.

Including her and Gareth.

"So we pursued," she explained. "The investigation eventually took us to Talyarkinash's lab, where we got our first big break. But Gareth, Talyarkinash, Morty, and Xiomber made their getaway, although not without some luck and surprise."

Like Eveth running into a Quarrie and losing her pocketcomm. And then deciding to pursue Gareth alone, into an alley, where he and Talyarkinash ambushed her. And escaped without anyone being hurt. More than their pride, anyway.

Or walking into a bar and threatening the owner with all manner of physical implications if he immediately didn't give her everything she wanted to know, with the alternative involving jail, or a hospital.

Or both.

"Kicking over anthills, Constable Baker?" one of the other Chaa spoke up. *Astray In Darkness* seemed to be his name. Or something like that. Religion had never been her strong suit, and she wasn't impressed enough to start now.

"I was in a hurry," she replied, turning her attention to a more interested participant, from the tone of his voice. "Time was running out if we wanted to stop all this before it got out of hand. Oh, sure, Jack's friends would have been able to have a field day, unraveling things patiently over the course of months, once we knew where to shine the light, but Gareth would have gotten away from us, and Sarzynski probably would have disappeared."

"So using violence, or at least the threat of it is an acceptable form of policing in the modern age?" the man(?) asked.

Eveth shrugged.

"One can always choose to cooperate with a police investigation instead," she fired back. "There are criminals we're talking about. They have already broken Accord by their actions, so they need to be watched, possibly even arrested and put in a small cell until they come to see the error of their ways, or are no longer a threat to their compatriots."

She felt a surge of anger come up from somewhere unexpected, deep inside.

It had been a day. It had been a week of days, and now she was facing a plethora of angry gods intent on killing her partner and wiping out his entire species because they were too lazy to fix things.

Or too incompetent, but you didn't necessary say that to a god. At least not to his face.

Astray In Darkness apparently had really good psychic ears. She felt his back come up like an angry cat as he watched her, ever so slightly, but he refrained from rising to her snarling challenge, contained, for now, just between the two of them.

"But you failed," the being glyphed at her solemnly.

"We did," she agreed. "By the time we had a lead on Talyarkinash Liamssen and Gareth, Maximus had already gotten there and captured both of them. Worse, the geneticist had already done her magic to the human, so now we had all that extra risk and danger thrown into the mix. And we got surprised and lost a firefight, Jack and I."

She actually felt the rage of a god touch her soul briefly as somebody extracted the next piece from her. They turned to their right, and suddenly two Warreth females and an older Nari man were hanging in the air, not far from Marc Sarzynski.

Unlike their polite handling of her and Talyarkinash, someone was playing rough. Eveth heard gurgles of pain and surprise from all three as they were manhandled into place.

Eveth snarled at the god.

That was still rape, as far as she was concerned.

"Maiair. Yooyar. Zorge," *Astray In Darkness* named them for the Court, and eternity. "You are broken failures. Poor examples of what the *Accord of Souls* was intended to become."

"Yeah?" Yooyar snapped at the Chaa. "And?"

Eveth nearly chuckled out loud at the Warreth woman's audacity, but then, what did they have to lose at this point? This wasn't going to be life in a prison cell. Not with these beings. There was going to be a house cleaning shortly.

Eveth suspected that it would be an ugly affair. At least for certain members of the audience.

Eveth got to watch as someone extracted glyphs from the two women a little more politely and displayed them for the others. The Nari male had apparently been sitting in the van, oblivious to the firefight behind him, even afterwards. She and Jack had gotten the drop on the two Warreth, but missed Maximus and let him sneak up on them.

The shot from the corner that got Jack. Her shot nearly nailing Maximus, but not enough to stop him. Both Warreth firing, the smaller one being the more deadly of the two.

Tossed bodily into the back of the van, along with Talyarkinash and Gareth. Transported to that secret warehouse where she and Jack were chained to a frame. Gareth more or less hung from another frame, because Maximus wanted to watch the man transform and see what Talyarkinash had done to him.

And Talyarkinash…

Eveth suppressed another growl. The Nari woman had regrown all the fur on her arm, but there was still a long, thin line of a scar visible underneath. Talyarkinash had kept the reminder, when she might have erased it with her science, because she wanted a souvenir of that night.

As if any of them actually needed something to remember what had happened.

The memories came also from Maximus now. Eveth could taste the extra layer of rage like frosting over them. That part warmed her soul, admittedly smaller than it should have been. The bad guys were also getting theirs tonight.

And they deserved it.

Eveth had been too groggy to remember much of the early part of the evening. Gareth had given everyone a good blow by blow account after that night, a result of Talyarkinash upgrading his excellent memory to be eidetic.

Gareth awakening first, dressed in white robes that seemed to bring with them some religious implications for the two men. Sarzynski on his throne, such as it was, but surrounded by his full Court of criminals.

At least those that had still believed in the man's power to that point.

Before…

Sarzynski waking Talyarkinash with a chemical smell, and then shaving a strip of fur off the Nari woman's arm. Before he stabbed her with his knife.

The rage that flowed back and forth between the two men like a river of lightning bolts between two magnetic poles as they screamed at each other. Two long-time friends, now at odds.

Worlds would fall before their battle was done.

Eveth glanced around the room at the truth of the words. Worlds were truly going to fall today. The *Accord of Souls* would be altered in ways that seemed impossible just yesterday.

A new future would be born tonight.

"Star Dragon," Eveth managed to say, loud enough that all eyes turned back to her.

The images displayed had been tinged with fear. Someone read her memories now and introduced them instead, since she had been awake enough at this point to witness the birth of a new life form.

A new symbol. Perhaps a new hope for the galaxy, in the face of Marc Sarzynski and his drive for *Empire*.

Gareth's scream of pure rage at that moment of transformation. The one that would have woken her anyway. Would have woken anyone in the building, since it was more than just audio waves.

The *Ascended Chaa* watched the man transform into something none of them had probably ever done before. Watched him break those chains. Take flight, pouring dragonfear into the souls of the assembled criminal underworld, where it would go on to infect planets like a virulent, new plague.

As intended.

And then Gareth started breathing fire.

Only now, watching with the added benefit of seeing the emotional impact that night had on the two Warreth women and the Nari male, did Eveth understand why Gareth hadn't just wiped them all out.

Would it have been better that night, for everyone involved if the human had chosen to destroy Sarzynski and Talyarkinash? Better for the entire galaxy?

She couldn't say. And that said a great deal. She hadn't realized how much she had come to respect the former career criminal, the Nari geneticist who had simply handed the Constabulary the keys to translate all her encoded records afterwards, so they could start the process of cleaning up *Hurquar*. Had even stood up to Jack, when the man wanted to throw her in a prison cell forever, because both Eveth and Jack knew that they would need Talyarkinash's help to understand Gareth.

When had that woman become such a friend?

"Star Dragon, why did you not destroy the human when you had the opportunity?" *Last Traveler* asked in a booming, angry voice.

"Because doing so would have killed my friend," Gareth said back in a tone so fundamentally calm that Eveth had to look over at the man. "Not Marc. Talyarkinash."

Eveth had had the same argument with the man five minutes later. And lost that one, too.

"One life lost, in balance for all of the rest," the being snapped.

"One friend given up, for no better reason than mere revenge?" Gareth countered. "I was raised better than that, *Chaa*."

As rebukes went, Eveth wasn't sure she had ever heard someone so solidly put into their place in so few words. But she felt the anger behind Gareth's tones. The Star Dragon wasn't far from the surface now.

She flashed back to the rage boiling off Gareth at that moment when they had proven beyond doubt that Gonquah had been building killer robots for Sarzynski. How hard he had worked to control it, in spite of wanting to unleash that impossible thing called *human anger*.

That thing that even the Chaa apparently feared.

"And I didn't let him go," Gareth continued in a snarl that almost made the air glow red. "The promise was one day's head start. That's all. His life that night, for that of the other three: Talyarkinash, Eveth, and Jackeith. One day. He got more, but only because it took longer than I expected to make my case to the Constabulary. However, his gang had been broken at that point. Dragonfear had served its purpose and was racing madly across the galaxy, taking criminals down or chasing them into their dens on world after world. And I never stopped chasing the man. *Will never stop.*"

Eveth felt a shiver. It seemed almost like a tide washing across the entire auditorium, touching every single being in the room, including the gods. Such was the power behind Gareth's words.

The rage.

The promise.

Something changed. She couldn't put her finger on it, but the room seemed to grow larger. And perhaps smaller at the same time.

Gareth was still Gareth, but it almost seemed like the Star Dragon had joined them in here, invisible, but present nonetheless.

Was that what it meant to be human? Among humans, Eveth had only ever met Gareth in person, and heard stories about Marc Sarzynski, but tonight she had met others. Pippa. Royston. Even the musician Ellen.

All of them had some manner of power about them that seemed lacking, compared to the rest of the chamber. At least the mortal parts.

"Last Traveler, is that why?" Eveth managed to cast her voice up into the maelstrom of the *Ascended Chaa* that were somehow above her, like witnesses up on a balcony, rather than down at ground floor. "Is that why you fear the humans?"

Everyone gasped.

ALL OF THE COMMUNION suddenly seemed close enough to touch, but they had never moved. Merely turned to look at a Prime Investigator named Eveth Baker.

But she understood now.

She and the others really weren't people to the Chaa. Those beings were already at least seventy thousand years old. Probably several times that amount, if she was reading them correctly with eyes that had been closed until now.

She and the others were merely facets of the *Accord of Souls*. Items on a checklist.

Not people with dreams.

Suddenly she was larger, but she had never moved. Someone had lifted her up to another place, somehow.

"Is that why humans were never admitted to the *Accord of Souls*?" she pressed, understanding what had triggered these gods into motion now.

Her voice contained no trepidation. That wasn't what Eveth Baker was about, but neither was the quaver mere curiosity.

"Because the humans had the potential to become you at some point?" Eveth let the inductive parts of her imagination fill in the gaps in the picture she had assembled in her mind. "So that they could join you in your quest, if they could somehow be kept isolated long enough to either mature, or wipe themselves out, as some others we have encountered have done?"

"You are correct, *Daughter of the Accord*," a new voice spoke up.

She turned to study the glyph of the one known simply as *Mountain*, even to its fellows.

Mountain. A thing of sturdy strength and beauty, but also a place from which you can fall if you are not careful. But if you do not, you can see sometimes forever, standing on those broad, strong shoulders.

Narrator of History spoke now, addressing herself to everyone who could hear her voice, which might be everyone alive.

"Twenty-nine Chitra ago, First Immortal **Awakened**," she said simply. "The Chaa were already a long-lived race at that point. Powerful with psionic ability, but the potential for more. She showed us the way."

They did not look all that different from the Vanir

in the images, the glyphs presented to the galaxy. Perhaps they had merely stripped away most of the psionic potential, when they modified the ones who chose not to become gods?

Those Left Behind. The Vanir, because they were no longer Chaa. And the Chaa left them with sixteen other species, uplifted to provide companionship, but also in need of protection, which was why so many Vanir seemed to gravitate into law enforcement.

Protecting the innocent, as Gareth had understood.

"Within a Chitra, many others Ascended, including much of *The Communion*," Narrator of History continued. "We were the first. *Last Traveler* was not the last to Ascend, but rather the last of *The Communion* to depart from the *Accord of Souls*, waiting for a time so that his comrades could leap ahead on their quest for the *Creator Who Gave Us Dreams*. But we did not choose to include humans into our construction."

"Why was that?" Eveth asked *Mountain*, rather than *Narrator To History*.

He seemed like the one who wanted to say something, when everyone else would have trusted their storyteller to handle the task.

The room fell silent. So silent Eveth wondered if the heartbeat she was hearing belonged to a Chaa, or perhaps the galaxy itself, somehow awake and listening in.

"Humans, then or now, are a violent species," *Mountain*'s voice sounded like nothing so much as an avalanche beginning to find its way to the valley below. "But that is a facet of their emotional depth, which is greater than all other sentient beings we have met, save the Chaa ourselves."

Eveth could hear the truth of those words. Gareth was possessed of an inherent power she did not understand, but knew to be a human thing not shared within the *Accord of Souls*.

Looking around, she saw something similar in Pippa. In Dr. Loughty. Even in Marc Sarzynski.

Induction. The ability to make leaps of fancy that span bottomless chasms where logic is stopped.

Eveth was an inductive detective. That was why they had paired her with Jack, the master of logic. At least that was the story she had been told. And it had been enough of the truth that she wasn't going to bicker on the finer points of the rest today. She had made it to Prime Investigator, which was really that thing she wanted most out of life.

But even being confronted by gods wasn't going to turn that off.

"Those others, the ones you destroyed," she said. "They lacked that potential, and were thus an ultimate threat. But humans, if they could be contained long enough, might grow into something else. What is that?"

In the room, a few dozen corporeal beings. An even dozen gods. A few thousand *Ascended Chaa*.

Eveth somehow felt the stare of the entire galaxy, every man, woman, and child, focused on her alone.

A moment of uncertainty passed between the gods she faced. Eveth wasn't sure if that made her feel better or scared her entirely out of her wits, that she could back-foot beings such as this.

The next moment, eyes seemed to turn sideways,

up on that platform, alighting on one of their number.

"To understand that, daughter, you must understand that which was destroyed," *Merciless* intoned gravely. "Perhaps it is time for their tale to be known."

MERCILESS

HE HAD NEVER TOLD the tale, even to his brother and sisters of *The Communion*. It was enough that the task was done. They did not need that stain on their own souls, when it came time to stand before *Eternity* and own the depth of this crime.

Modern Chitra called him *Merciless*, but in an earlier age they had teased him good-naturedly as *Restless*. Forever bouncing from place to place, seeking the clues that would lead them all to a higher understanding of the *Creator's Vision For All*.

Restless had found an advanced, alien species. Given the exacting nature of hindsight, he had wondered if the *First Cause* had intentionally put the Tronafora almost exactly opposite Humanity as the galaxy spun. One hundred and seventy-eight degrees, and only slightly closer to the galactic core.

Two more powerful, dangerous species that would stand in the path of the Chaa, and their goal of spanning the entire disk into a single, harmonious entity, populated by nearly forty intelligent species, eventually.

Thus might even the true gods have a sense of humor, black though it might be.

Merciless reached into the Pandora's Box he kept close to his soul, where the glyphs might be stored deep and never shared. He had only expected to share these memories with the Originator at the moment when he would be judged for his ultimate fate.

But he was *Merciless*. That title included ruthlessness. And Duty.

Merciless paused for one infinitesimal moment to nod to the Star Dragon. *Merciless* understood a duty that required you to give up all things for a greater good. The human Gareth nodded back, blood brothers separate from all the rest in this room.

He glyphed the first image of the Tronafora that any being had known six Chitra ago. Because the Vanir Constable Eveth Baker had been the one to ask, he Witnessed her reaction, as an measure of the rest.

They were a bipedal species, that still being the most efficient mechanism to move and still retain extra limbs that could be specialized into tool use. Baker found them spindly and a bit awkward, but that was her own estimate, having never seen them move.

A fast Vanir might outrun a Tronafora, in a race.

The species was lightly scaled, with three horns on their head in a manner that might span the space between Yuudixtl and Traakna, except that Tronafora were nearly Vanir height.

What separated them from all the other species that the Chaa had encountered, intelligent or not, was their culture, which had erased all religious overtones or references and embraced a purely mechanistic atheism almost as extreme as *Restless* found mathematically possible.

No greater afterlife existed in their worldview, where the *Creator Who Forgives* might judge them on the accomplishments of their lives and separate the worthy from those destined to whatever hell awaited. Each was merely a cog in a faceless machine, struggling constantly not with ethics and philosophy, but to attain, sustain, and expand one's personal power, generally at the cost to others from whom such power was of necessity stolen.

A ruthless pyramid of conquerors who found no value in any other species, and had discovered the same mathematics that had allowed them to escape the prison of their clockwork homeworld and begin slowly colonizing nearby systems.

Merciless showed the assembly image after image of the world known as *Bota Fori*. Gray skies thick with smoke and pollutants from the factories, hard at work putting out ever newer and more powerful machines designed to kill. Factories and barracks covering every bit of surface. Landdragons lumbering on four legs with beam cannon for eyes. Skydragons to scout, with smaller beams, plasma breath, and adamantine claws to pounce and rake.

The Communion had met *In Congress Assembled* when *Restless* had returned with his news. The *Accord of Souls* had already been planned and was in the process of being born. The Tronafora had been missed, almost hidden in their distant corner of the circular galaxy, because the entire species gave off almost no psychic emanations whatsoever.

Humans, for comparison, as *Merciless* put the two side by side for all to see, contained almost enough psionic capacity for both species. And humans had yet to move past stone tools to anything so simple as metal, while the Tronafora had already fully hived the surface of their own world with metal and stone buildings and fortifications, and expanded to five others, one of which had not been empty when the invaders arrived.

Merciless let his anger color this glyph. To do otherwise would inflict harm on himself that was unnecessary. His kin would understand and think him no ill. The corporeal could not grasp, anyway.

Pr'Taxxu.

It had been a lovely, green and blue world. Once. By the time *Restless* discovered it, the planet's hiving was nearly complete, and he could only listen to the fading echo of the people who might have grown up to become the Taxxa.

Had there been any left alive at that point.

There were only Tronafora there now. *Restless* and the others had come too late to prevent a xenocide. At that point, even a geocide was imminent, as every native plant and animal was slowly being destroyed, replaced by things brought instead from *Bota Fori*.

"Most species are left alone," he spoke aloud for the first time. "Time will cause them to evolve into something more socially acceptable, or they will reach one of several biological or technological bottlenecks in their development and cease to exist as a viable species. We have witnessed this many times, and have the archaeological record of other species that might have reached our stage of development had they not."

"Were you the first?" a voice emerged from the crowd of corporeal beings below.

Merciless let himself ruminate on the topic for a long moment. *First Immortal* and *Great Docent* were the oldest of their kind, but *Bowsprit* and *Glory in Sunrise* had been the farthest roaming, along with the creature once known as *Restless*.

"We have found no evidence of other such *Ascended* in this galaxy," he finally said, carefully hedging his words.

"In this galaxy?" the creature asked, apparently reading the finer shading on the glyph better than *Merciless* had expected.

He turned to study the creature. One of the humans. A female. Daughter of another present, and emotionally mated to the Star Dragon.

Philippa Adeline Loughty. *Pippa*, to those who knew her. A woman thwarted by her culture, but unwilling to settle for failure. Her brilliance, while masked, approached that of her father in places. Her empathy for others outdid any of the human men present, and sat at a special, elevated level equaled only by the other human female, Ellen Denise Ames, leader of the musical gestalt.

"We have, by now, traversed roughly seventeen thousand other galaxies to some extent," *Merciless* told the woman. "In others, there has been some evidence that such beings as ourselves once existed. Some have galaxy-spanning civilizations, such as the *Accord of Souls* will eventually become, while others have left behind traces that such projects were attempted, but later failed."

"How does a galaxy-spanning civilization fail?" Pippa asked. "I could see on a single world, as resource depletion or warfare might do the trick. Even a single, unexpected meteor might unleash a cataclysmic, extinction-level event sufficient to undo higher civilization. How can that happen on this scale?"

Truly, the humans were more advanced than *Merciless* had expected. And he gathered, from the reactions of his kin, that others had discovered the same today.

It was good.

"On your own world, life exploded and then thrived for millions of years," *Merciless* brought up images from her own mind of great lizards that had once roamed. "But in your case, they have been gone for more than sixty thousand Chitra. We have only been **Awakened** for twenty-nine Chitra. Two hundred and ninety thousand human years. And even that is not as long as your species has existed. Who else might have evolved, *Ascended*, and departed even so recently as a thousand Chitra ago?"

He watched the woman nod her understanding, which surprised *Merciless* so much that he invaded her mind to see what it was that she saw. A moment later, both *Astray in Darkness* and *Last Traveler* silently rebuked him, and *Merciless* relaxed his hold on the creature's mind, allowing her to share, rather than forcing her to submit to his will.

How much have we forgotten, if we have lost even our manners? Merciless wondered at himself.

But she did understand. Such a primitive species, all things considered, and she understood that the galactic scale was just a matter of size over the planetary, and thus civilizations themselves could evolve so far that they eventually tired and died.

Merciless thanked her for teaching him such understanding and returned to the Tronafora.

No others of his kin could tell this tale, as none had been close enough to actually witness it firsthand. *The Decision* had been made, to expunge an entire sentient species, as one might cut out a cancer to save the infested being. Or galaxy.

Six worlds. Hived over to provide a home for the Tronafora conquering machines. To stand as beacons for the various fleets seeking out new worlds to take. New species to eliminate.

New evil to be done in the name of whatever Tronafora culture venerated in their militant, mechanistic atheism.

Restless had found them. Had brought them to the notice of *The Communion*. He volunteered to end them, alone, so that none of the others might have such a crime to bear.

And it was a crime. An entire species wiped from existence and memory, merely to eliminate the risk to the fledgling *Accord of Souls* that was even then merely a dream of the two cousins, *Magistrate* and *Uplifter*.

Restless became *Merciless*. The assembled galaxy watched his transformational memories. *Bota Fori* destroyed first. *O'Pequiz. Xani. Ribble. Telea Mani.* Finally *Pr'Taxxu.*

Other worlds where the explorers had not yet begun to Hive with their militant civilization were left alone, once the infection of Tronafora was removed bodily from their solar systems. Fleets exploring were picked up and cast into nearby stars to purify them in fire. Tronafora were hunted down and eliminated.

Merciless.

An entire culture that evaporated in an afternoon, leaving only six dead stars behind as mute testimony. Monuments to…something. Even he wasn't sure what to call it.

But the task was done.

Around him, the *Ascended Chaa* fell silent, shocked to witness the thing, when most had been sufficient to know it had been done.

"So you failed," Pippa announced.

DAUGHTER

SHE COULD NOT CONTAIN herself any longer. Pippa had watched these powerful beings, proto-gods, perhaps, interacting with Gareth and Father. With the Constables and aliens all brought here for judgment.

Her words echoed off of whatever metaphysical ceiling might contain them, but she watched them sting the one known as *Merciless* the hardest.

"Failed?" he demanded in a soft tone that still contained all the rage he had internalized, that which allowed him to become *Merciless*.

"Failed," Pippa said. "Yes, you committed a most thorough xenocide, I'm sure. Eliminated every trace of the Tronafora from place or history. Wiped the slate utterly clean on six worlds. *What did you gain?*"

She couldn't help the anger that bubbled up. Her hands were still bound to the Nari woman Talyarkinash, and felt the woman's recoil of shock and dismay. Through her, Fatima as well, a linking of females across three separate species.

"We protected the *Accord of Souls*," one of the other Chaa spoke. *Uplifter*, she thought, but Pippa couldn't be sure.

"No, you destroyed a threat to it," she challenged his interpretation. "One of them, apparently. Why did you not go ahead and complete the task? Why were humans not eliminated then, before they rose to be a challenge?"

As audacity went, Pippa quailed inside, but she would not be stilled.

She could see it now, in ways that perhaps even these gods could not. These creatures were reactive, not active. They displayed such a muddled thinking that she was offended by it. And let them know it.

"We did not see humans as a threat," *Narrator To History* spoke up. "Until today, that held true. Indeed, they needed to be kept isolated, but that was for their own good. Until your father, humans could not reach the *Accord of Souls* without assistance."

"He did not even seek you, until your kind, your grandchildren, meddled in our existence," Pippa sneered at the being. "And yet, the punishment will be ours to pay, and not theirs."

"It will not fall solely on your kind," *Uplifter* replied with a special anger it its voice.

"So humans are so great a threat to the *Accord* that they must be eliminated, because otherwise the people of the *Accord* will play with matches again?" Pippa asked the being a sharp tone. "Why do you not teach them not to play with matches in the first place?"

"Your kind have had five Chitra to develop and evolve, human," *Uplifter* snarled down at her. "We left you alone then, rather than incorporate you into the *Accord of Souls* because we believed that it would be possible. But we are gathered now to witness how badly that decision went wrong."

"No, you are here to gloat on the superiority of your culture and technology that you can do anything you want, to whomever you desire, and nothing but *God Himself* can probably stop you," Pippa let her anger lash at the man. "That does not make you better. It makes you infantile."

Suddenly, Pippa came to understand what it meant to have twelve, angry proto-gods focus themselves on you. Someone grabbed hold of her mind again, less politely than before. They squeezed, ever so slightly. Not enough to hurt, but sufficient that her thoughts and memories were exposed.

Hopefully, nobody but these gods could truly read her soul and all the secrets contained therein.

She felt herself sifted like flour, *Forty-niners* seeking every flake of gold that the riverbank might surrender to patience and will.

Finally, they let her go. Somehow, each of her own hands was now being held by the other two women, a triangle of support between Grace, Nari, and Human.

"Guilt is a human thing born of fear," *Speaker For The Communion* enunciated clearly as the being returned to their platform to scowl down at the ephemeral.

Pippa smiled at him. At all of them. She picked out the one she wanted and bored her mind in on him with her own ruthlessness.

"And yet," she crowed. "*Merciless* would not accept help in his xenocide, because of your overwhelming fear, all of you, that you will have to face *God The Creator* one of these days with such a stain on your souls. If that is not guilt, pray tell me what word I should use instead to describe your failure?"

Razor blades covered in honey still cut. She could see metaphorical blood dripping up there as they listened to her.

They had read her mind, these twelve. Seen her ideas, her suggestion, possibly her future, if she had such a thing.

"What you suggest as an alternative is so impractical as to be nearly impossible," *Glory In Sunrise* spoke now. Unlike many of the others, she glyphed from a primarily female point of view, although Pippa understood now that to be Chaa was to contain within one's self the ability to take on any form.

Even then, some had been born with male tendencies that colored their behavior and thought processes, just as *Glory In Sunrise* and *Narrator To History*, among others, had been born female.

If you could use such a verb to describe the arrival of one of these proto-gods, back in the distant history when they were merely nigh-immortal wizards of great power and vision.

"My idea is nearly impossible?" Pippa picked out the woman and smiled coldly at her. "From a species that can pick up a black hole and drop it anywhere they want, as a way to punish upstart species?"

Pippa had a moment of sadness overtake her, as she considered her mother and how Elizabeth might have handled these beings. Mother would have been even less flexible than Father, and in that Pippa strove to emulate the woman she had not kissed goodnight in nearly two decades.

Elizabeth wouldn't have taken a gram of shit off these people. Pippa wasn't about to start.

Around her, gasps, from mouths human as well as other. One did not sass gods, apparently. At least in their worldview.

Pippa had never allowed a man to dictate things to her, including Father. If these proto-gods were going to kill her, to kill every single one of her friends, she would meet them on her feet, not her knees.

Suddenly, the triangle of power was broken as Talyarkinash and Fatima let go of the hands they had been holding together, even as they somehow retained their grip on her. Pippa thought they were moving away from her, but they were each turning to stand at her side, joining her in facing off with these beings, these angry children who expected to bully people out of their way.

Tough.

"What would it gain?" *Mountain* spoke in a voice like an earthquake reaching up for the surface of the planet.

"Time," Pippa fixed her terrible gaze on the Chaa and glyphed at him. "You had all expected humanity to reach a special place in another Chita. To be able to join you in your grand quest, your mad adventure, even as you guaranteed that no other species in this galaxy would ever even come close. This would give you time to find out if that is possible."

"And the cost?" *Mountain* asked.

"A few worlds, a few millennia," she replied. "You, who have already spent nine Chitra exploring seventeen thousand galaxies cannot be that greedy, can you?"

Dead silence. Even the grave might make more noise.

Pippa found the light in here different, as though the room had changed, or the galaxy. One could never be too sure, with dreamers like these involved.

"The *Ascended Chaa* will retire to consider this proposal from the human, Philippa Adeline Loughty," *Speaker For The Communion* announced in a voice that seemed to echo across eternity.

And just like that, they were gone. All of them.

Pippa looked up and all those faces that had been on the platform had vanished. All the lesser beings that had been floating like ghosts went with them.

Only the ephemeral remained behind.

"What have you done, Daughter?" Father was there.

He looked like he wanted to hug her, but held back, no doubt a little awed by the circumstances, but also by the two menacing shield maidens holding her flanks. Pippa stepped forward and hugged him instead.

"Maybe I have found a way to save us," she whispered.

BROTHERS

GARETH FELT THE CHAA LEAVE, in ways he didn't think he could explain to the others. But he also wasn't just one person, anymore. Around him, he could feel the Star Dragon flying, almost as if they were separating into two beings, at least for today.

He would miss that thing, if he were indeed to lose it, but if it would make things better, then he would be happy for the loss.

Still, the hands holding him in place were gone now, as well. He could move without anyone stopping him.

Gareth felt his head turn to the left. One Vanir form, surrounded by several others, not all that far away from him.

Marc.

He took a step. Watched Marc suddenly freed from whatever cage had held him up in the air, so that they stood eye to eye watching.

Gareth reached a hand out tentatively as he approached the barrier separating Marc and his gang from the rest of the room. Probably a wise choice, especially if the Chaa were truly as gone as they seemed.

Still he walked close. Watched Marc do the same, even as his associates, the Warreth sisters Maiair and Yooyar, and the Nari Zorge, stepped back, away from him.

But for the thing between them, they might talk alone for the first time in nearly four years.

Behind him, Gareth felt the rest of the room also seem to recede, as if everyone understood that this conversation needed to be private.

"Hello, Marc," Gareth said simply.

"Gareth," the man answered in a tone more weary than wary. "I'm sorry that it had to come to this."

"And I as well," Gareth replied. "But I don't suppose that there really were any other options, were there?"

"No," Marc said. "It had grown too big to be contained in just the Solar System. Or even the *Accord of Souls*. Eventually, either you would have found a way to stop me, or I would have conquered the galaxy and created a human-dominated Empire."

"Why?" Gareth asked simply, that one syllable containing all those years, all the arguments never had.

All the possibilities gone.

"I couldn't handle being second best, Gareth," Marc said. "I used to think you knew that, but I've learned more in the last hour than I had in the previous twenty-nine years. Until now, I never truly understood that it was never a competition to you.

Or rather, the only person you were competing with was Gareth."

"Yes," Gareth said. "I wanted to be the best me I could. I'm sorry it took all this for you to understand. What could we have accomplished, if you had?"

Marc laughed lightly, suddenly sounding more like the man Gareth remembered from their youth rather than the criminal warlord intent on conquering the universe.

"Eventually, I would have probably become the Sky Marshal of Sky Patrol," Marc said. "That was one of the enticements they dangled in front of me when it became clear that I was leaving. You never would have wanted the job, so it wouldn't have been a competition."

"No," Gareth nodded. "I would have fought tooth and nail if they ever wanted to promote me past Senior Special Agent, because that would have meant a desk job. Not my style."

"And it really wasn't you, in the end, Gareth," Marc said.

Gareth watched the man's eyes wander back over his shoulder, but he didn't need to glance to know that Marc was looking at Pippa, wandering mentally back to a moment where she had chosen him instead.

Again, how much better might the world have been? Gareth would have been heart-broken and crestfallen, but he also knew that he would have gotten over it eventually. Somehow.

Marc never had. And it no longer mattered.

Their eyes locked again after a moment. Gareth could see all the pain of his memories in there, but there was also a new resolve.

"If we hadn't gotten ourselves into this mess, I

might have even found myself a new Empress from among the humans on *Earth*," Marc said. "I had found a template, the perfect woman, but she wasn't human, so she couldn't help with my long-term plans. And then she went and betrayed me."

It was Gareth's turn to let his eyes find a horizon and contemplate. He knew who Marc was talking about. And he agreed.

"Talyarkinash would have been perfect for you," Gareth said. "The old Talyarkinash, that is. From before."

"What did they do to her?" Marc's concern was genuine, with a tiny flare of real anger underneath.

"She had to reinvent herself into someone else when I came along," Gareth said with as much sincere honesty as he could press into the words. "When she was captured by the Constables and given the choice to cooperate with them or rot in a prison cell for the rest of her life. But she would have made a great mate for you. She has been an exceptional friend when I needed one."

Marc nodded.

Gareth knew he should feel something more. Some rage or jealousy, but they had moved past it all, it seemed, the two of them. They could just stand here and talk, like two old friends in a bar who haven't seen each other in several years, catching up before returning to their separate lives.

Except nobody would ever return to their old lives. Most of their friends wouldn't have life shortly. At least he hoped he had made a good enough impression on people like Grodray and Baker. And on Talyarkinash.

They would be the only memory of him tomorrow.

"So why were you on *Earth*, Marc?" Gareth asked.

"It was the last place I expected anyone to look for me," the man chuckled. "And I had enough contacts there that they could hide us for a while, and enough wealth to get what I needed. But it never would have been enough for me. I would have eventually recruited an army of gunmen and tried to conquer the *Accord of Souls*. That's just the way I'm wired these days."

Gareth nodded this time. He could recognize such a stark truth. Even *Earth* wouldn't have been enough for Marc.

How are you going to keep them on the farm, after they've been to gay Paris?

"And I did need to find myself an Empress," Marc continued. "Someone like Pippa, but more ruthless. Or like Talyarkinash, but human so that I could start a Royal House. I had planned to live forever, once I found the right geneticist. At least several millennia, rather than decades. I would have reshaped everything in my image, like Machiavelli always demanded."

"What would you have done when the Chaa came back and objected?" Gareth asked with a smile.

"Yesterday, they were just a myth, old friend," Marc smiled back. "Fables told to children to keep them in line, like the bogeyman. I would have spit in their faces, and they would have probably snuffed me out, and then spent a century undoing everything I had been trying to build. But what the hell do us pitiful humans know?"

They shared a chuckle at that. Yes, it would have

played out about like that.

How do you plan for angry gods to return? You don't. Not rationally. And it wasn't like there was anything he or Marc could have done to stop beings of such enormous power.

But time was growing short. The Chaa would return soon, from wherever they had gone to talk without the children listening in.

"Marc, I'm sorry it turned out like this," Gareth said earnestly. "I wish we could have found a way to make it work, back then, or somehow since."

"And I as well," Marc said, his eyes growing sad and somber. "The follies of youth we can never undo. The choices we can never go back and make right. But these Ghosts of Christmas Past, Present, and Future will not lead us to the sort of happily-ever-after that you find in the vids."

"I am still honored that you were my friend, even if we lost that later," Gareth said.

He held up a hand and placed it on the shield that separated them. There was no greater symbol for all of this that he could find.

"And I you, Gareth," Marc replied, placing his own hand opposite Gareth's, separated by nearly a foot of invisible barrier. "Perhaps in our next incarnations we will get it right. Or at least closer."

"Next incarnations, Marc?" Gareth chided him. "You don't think we aren't both immediately going to hell for this?"

"Were I still of your faith, I would expect that, Gareth," Marc replied. "You would not, for reasons I don't think you have the emotional capacity to understand, but that's fine. I went elsewhere, looking for something to fill in that hollow spot in my soul. I found a militant form of Buddhism that spoke to me well enough."

"Did it bring you joy?" Gareth asked.

He watched Marc look inward for a moment before the man nodded.

"It did."

"Then I'm happy for you," Gareth said. And he meant it. "All I ever wanted was for my friends to find joy. Even you, afterwards. I never stopped hoping that you would find your way out of that darkness."

"All it took was the intervention of a cadre close enough to gods that nobody could tell the difference," Marc laughed. "And the destruction of everything either of us had ever known, ever loved. So when you're in heaven, and I'm being reborn, maybe we can both work to make the universe a better place."

"I hope so, my friend," Gareth said. "I do not ever intend to stop trying."

Marc nodded and stepped back, letting his hand fall to his side. Gareth did the same.

They would be destroyed by the Chaa shortly enough, and none of it would matter, but he had at least had a chance to talk to his old friend again.

It was enough.

Around him, Gareth felt the arrival of the Chaa, all of them, like an invisible squall line passing overhead, bringing with it a change in temperature and pressure, as the impending storm prepared to take you.

"People Of The Earth, you will hear me," *Speaker For The Communion* called to all corners of the galaxy again, just as he had before. "The time has come."

DEFENDER

ROYSTON FELT THE CHAA APPROACH. Like the others, he had been standing back, watching Gareth and Marc perhaps finally come to peace, even as they were separated by a barrier none could crack.

The two men could finally talk as equals. Hopefully expressing those things that had been buried for so long.

But the moment passed.

"People Of The Earth, you will hear me," *Speaker For The Communion* commanded. "The time has come."

Royston slid away from the others, as interesting as such alien people were and as pleasant as their earlier conversations had been. All eyes had been watching Marc and Gareth, breaths held so tight that no noise would interrupt.

The Gods were returning.

Royston approached the two men. They had found peace, it was obvious. Either would have been acceptable as a son-in-law five years ago, when such a thing was possible and Royston had called in every favor he was owed to know the background of the two.

Just like that, it was as if the intervening years had passed.

Thus do we all grow up, he mused.

The barrier separating them was present for Marc and Gareth, but Royston stepped right up to that point and apparently through it, as if even it understood that the time for violence was over and the shield no longer necessary.

"Gareth, Marc, come," he ordered the two, surprising both men by taking one of their hands and pulling them back to the center of things.

"How…?" Marc started to say, but Royston just smiled at him.

"It is time to deal with this as adults, young men," he said back sternly.

He could do that. Royston Loughty was old enough to be their father, and had been a Special Agent of the Earth Force Sky Patrol, back in his highly-classified younger days, before Elizabeth.

Neither man resisted as Royston pulled them along, much like the triangle of power that Pippa had formed with Fatima and the Nari woman Talyarkinash earlier, when his amazing daughter had challenged the gods themselves to behave.

Glancing back, the group of criminals that had attended Marc followed, sucked into Royston's wake but still protected from harm. If you were about to watch someone be executed, why bother stepping in?

The group did not split into facets, as he had expected, but merged seamlessly. Everyone understood that the time for violence was done.

The completion of all things was upon them.

Pippa stood front and center, glancing back at him in surprise and awe as her triangle of power matched his: Talyarkinash and Fatima standing at her wings, just as Gareth and Marc did his.

Chevrons aimed at the gods like arrows ready to be loosed.

"The *Ascended Chaa* have undertaken to discuss your proposal, Pippa Loughty," *Speaker For The Communion* announced. "The vote was the barest majority opposed, but even *The Communion* recognizes that pure democracy is not the method by which such a grave situation should be resolved. We would hear your dreams in your own words, that the vote may be swayed to a more secure and permanent majority."

Royston wanted to speak, but it was not his place. He had brought the two most dangerous poles of power into alignment, and perhaps that was enough. With the musician Ellen, the four of them might represent the most psionically powerful humans in existence right now.

"You destroyed the Tronafora, rather than let them continue expanding," Pippa observed in a slow, teaching voice. "Their militant atheism ran counter to everything you believed as a culture, so I feel that such anger colored your emotions too much."

Royston wondered if she had picked up the same shades as he from the glyphs *Merciless* had communicated. Perhaps she was a fifth part of their whole, and he had never truly appreciated that his daughter was his equal in so many ways.

It would be necessary to correct his behavior if they managed to survive this. Pippa truly was his peer. She should become his intellectual partner in all things, and not a mere assistant, even on paper.

Earth Force could get stuffed.

"They would have eventually sought to conquer the entire galaxy and subsume it beneath their Hives," *Merciless* replied grimly.

"That is entirely possible," Pippa agreed. "But with all your power, I have yet to see any hint of true precognition among you. You can estimate and theorize, but none of you can pierce the veil and actually see the future."

Royston felt a ripple of mild surprise roll across the *Ascended Chaa* as if such a thing had never even been considered. Perhaps there were limits to their godhead.

What would today have been like, had the Oracle at Delphi been able to advise these Olympians?

"So, yes, they would have tried," Pippa continued. "Or perhaps not. Perhaps an encounter with truly sentient aliens, rather than the verging-on-intelligent Taxxu, might have caused their society to recoil and evolve. *We cannot know.*"

"We cannot know," several of *The Communion* echoed, as if a call and response of the Kirk.

Royston could see fault lines emerge up there. Destroyers and Protectors, wavering back and forth on the decision to eradicate Humanity. It had been a razor-thin thing, he could tell.

"You cannot know what might have happened to them or to Humanity, irredeemably confronted with the greater galaxy and true gods," Pippa said, turning from left to right to take them all in as Royston watched with pride. His daughter, standing in for all humans. And Earth Force barely recognized that women might have something useful to contribute to science, to say nothing of politics. Fools.

"But you also have it in your power to refrain today, that you might find out," Pippa continued.

"We have heard your proposal, Pippa Loughty," *Speaker For The Communion* replied. "The Communion is split evenly on the idea, not because we do not see the merit of it, but because of the scope of potential power that it represents, and the cost to us. Explain yourself."

"I already know that you have the power to interrupt wormholes," Pippa said. "Gareth, Eveth, and Jackeith were in such a structure at the moment you blocked it, extracted them, and returned the rest of their team to their starting point. Such was the glyph you shared when announcing this Court."

"That is an active act," *Speaker For The Communion* said. "It requires a watcher to intercept such a thing."

"True," Pippa nodded. "But why can you not set up such a structure in space and power it with your will, or perhaps some psionic device you cause to be constructed. This was a technological advancement of yours before it was a mental one."

"Humans will not accept a cage," *Astray In Darkness* spoke up now. "Such a thing will cause them to redouble their effort to escape and return to being a threat, trebled now with the understanding that there are ranges out there denied to them. And people that could be conquered. Worlds looted. Technological advancements beyond their wildest dreams."

"Thus are humans engineers," *Glory in Sunrise*'s mirth seemed to infect everyone, both gods and the ephemeral below her. "Tell them a thing is impossible and watch them prove you wrong."

Royston could not debunk her theory. Look at what he had done when challenged by Pippa that his understanding of physics was insufficient.

"But if the cage is large enough, it might give the humans time to expand into the galaxy and find themselves," Pippa's voice took on a softer tone now. Not pleading, but invoking perhaps. "If there is an entire sandbox into which they might play, perhaps it will be enough to contain them. You yourselves expected it to take another Chitra before humans were evolved enough to approach. We have not even possessed metal-working technology for a full Chitra. What could we do with as much as another Chitra to explore one small corner of the galaxy, secure that we have it to ourselves. What art could we create?"

"And later, the humans would still be entirely contained, if it became necessary to eliminate them," *Merciless* offered in the most practical voice Royston thought he had ever heard.

"Why do you propose fifty light-years, Pippa Loughty?" *Speaker For The Communion* inquired in his magisterial voice.

"If I remember my studies correctly, a sphere fifty light-years across, centered on my Solar System, contains roughly fourteen hundred star systems, and approximately two thousand stars, when you factor in how common binary systems are," Pippa said. "And there are nearly one hundred and fifty stars similar enough to our own that they should have inhabitable planets around them."

"You are correct, but two of them already possess

advanced lifeforms that may yet evolve into beings that could join the *Accord of Souls* at a later date," *Narrator Of History* noted.

"So you would not form a perfect sphere," Pippa nodded. "You should still be able to erect and maintain a barrier that keeps humans in. Or out, as it were. The *Accord of Souls* would be protected, including future worlds you wished to admit. The human xenocide is at worst delayed. But at best, humans will evolve into someone that could eventually become a partner to the Chaa in their quest. Any you will go to meet God without an unnecessary stain on your souls."

"It will not work," *Mountain* announced. "As *Astray in Darkness* notes, humans will spend all their time trying to break out. One of us would have to maintain a constant, eternal vigil to prevent that."

"Not necessarily," Royston spoke up now.

He couldn't tell if the ideas were his own, or somehow flowed from one of the men with him. He wasn't even sure they were three separate beings now, rather than one composite gestalt that had formed under the pressure of the situation.

Like a second diamond, after the one Pippa had formed.

What would advanced humans be capable of, once the species got there? Royston didn't know, but he had half a dozen examples from which he might theorize.

"Speak, Father of Pippa," *Mountain* challenged.

Royston understood that the being was seeking a technical solution, and not just a sociological one, so he reached deep to tap the power suddenly at his command, unsure if it was Marc or Gareth offering hints. Probably both of them.

"Yes, I agree," Royston nodded in general to the Chaa. "A simple barrier a millimeter thick will fail quickly in its intended purpose. As a human, I would build a platform capable of sailing through the wall until I could set myself up on the other side and start my mischief again."

They had all seen the failure of such a solution immediately, but nobody here was apparently as sneaky as Marc, and Gareth, truth be told, to circumvent.

"Make the suppressor a light-year thick," Royston offered as a solution. "Humans do not have the capability, with our modern, chemical rockets, to traverse that distance in anything less than generations anyway."

"Even for us, the power requirements would be astronomical," *Mountain*'s voice almost contained a sneer, the first emotion Royston could remember coming from the being.

"Not necessarily," *Merciless*, of all people, spoke, echoing Royston's earlier words. "True, to relocate the number of black holes necessary to power such a shielding would greatly disrupt the gravitational tides of galactic plane, but we could also rely on a network of red and white dwarf stars. The result would not be uniformly spherical, but would also be more easily maintained for perhaps as long as a Chitra, before enough stars drifted to open gaps in the shielding effect."

"Is this your logic or your guilt speaking?" *First Immortal* asked, joining the conversation for the first time. "Are we hearing hope or shame?"

Royston had heard *First Immortal* referred to earlier as one of the female-born Chaa, but this powerful being sounded almost like the Goddess/Mother that all primitive cultures on *Earth* had worshipped in the beginning. There was nothing soft or compliant in those tones or glyphs. This was the Crone of ancient religions.

In that, she almost sounded like Pippa.

"Both, I would expect," *Merciless* answered honestly. "One cannot be separated from the other at this point in history. Is not one crime sufficient to take to our *Final Judgment*?"

And that, right there, was why it was perhaps necessary and acceptable for the Chaa to have destroyed the Tronafora. Royston had read the being's glyphs and understood that primitive species to have suppressed all religious belief. Doing so, like the various *Industrialisms* of the Twentieth Century always left man empty and hollow, for what was he without ethics?

What was any creature without an ethical structure upon which he could frame his actions? Scientists had long failed to provide an adequate demarcation between man and the higher animals. Many so-called lesser creatures had language. Had beliefs.

Only a few had ever been shown to have ethics. To look up at the scientist and say *"This is I will not do, because it is* wrong."

Thankfully, proposals by *Earth* scientists to uplift such creatures to a level that might rival humans had been turned down again and again as *Unethical*.

Let them evolve their own way, into the thing that

they should be rather than forcing them to meet our standards.

But then, wasn't that what the Chaa had attempted, so long ago? Uplift sixteen. Modify the seventeenth. Ignore most of the rest.

Hope that Humanity would find its own way.

Interestingly, Royston felt one of the Chaa extract from his gestalt and then from Pippa's a map of the near systems to Earth. At least as he understood them. One of the professional astronomers working at the Arsenal, with Luna providing a shadow against various radiation pollution from Earth itself, could have given them a more precise mapping, but if this was decided upon, the Chaa would handle it themselves anyway.

They wanted to know that it could be done. And done with efficiency and cost-effectiveness tossed in, so that one of them wasn't on duty to maintain it constantly.

Royston watched an image take shape above them, like a massive hologram, except this was entirely in his mind, as he understood it.

Just as it was in the mind of every human in existence, down to the smallest infant that might grow up to someday be an astronomer, a ship's captain, or an explorer.

It was not a perfect sphere. Once such an elegant solution was no longer necessary, it took on a more mechanical appearance.

No, better to describe it as a series of giant, transparent snowballs surrounding the *Earth* at a distance and enclosing it in a bumpy box. There was enough overlap in all places that the structure would appear to hold water.

And humans.

"Is this a task worth doing?" *Seeker For The Knee Of God* broke zir silence.

Unlike the others, this Chaa's voice contained no clues that might suggest a gender. Not that it was machine-like, but rather, so androgynous that it might be both genders at once.

When you controlled your form, anything was possible, limited only by your imagination and your need.

Look at the Star Dragon, for example.

Nobody answered the question posed, at least not where he could hear it.

Royston had a feeling that the *Ascended Chaa* were voting, in some secondary cloak room hidden from the ephemeral creatures. Voting again, perhaps.

Shifting like tides in response to the case made by Pippa to save her species, if that could be possible.

Like Gareth, Royston could live with having to be executed today, if not everything else was lost.

"The vote is amended," *Speaker For The Communion* announced as the *Ascended Chaa* returned. "*Merciless* and *Astray In Darkness* will cause the barrier to come into being, and power it sufficient for half a Chitra, at which time *The Communion* will reconvene."

Everyone understood the dark overtones of his voice, a rip current threatening to overwhelm you and drag you to a watery death at sea. Humans, you have five thousand years to get their act together and form a more perfect union.

Or perish.

It would not be his problem, dead for so long by

then that those humans might have forgotten his name.

Looking back, the progress over the last five thousand years did give Royston hope. It had only been thirty-six centuries since Homer's Ilium had fallen. Fifty centuries of time more or less encompassed written, human history, dating from the first writing systems attributed to the ancient Sumerians.

Where would another fifty centuries find us?

It was good. He and his friends had just saved billions of humans, potentially trillions, from extinction.

"Now we will address the criminals among us, and their punishments," *Speaker For The Communion* continued in a voice that filled this room with dread.

FIREMAN

MORTY FELT the gaze of that old bastard on the stage center on him.

Sure, start with me, you sanctimonious shit. I started it all, didn't I?

"Morty the Yuudixtl, your crimes, as you note, are the most significant, because without your efforts and genius, none of the rest of this situation could have occurred," *Speaker For The Communion* began.

Many of the other Chaa growled at him as well. He couldn't really blame them. Nobody likes to have to come into work on their day off just because somebody else screwed something up so badly that only a monumental effort will salvage things before the shit comes completely unraveled.

Not even gods.

Morty took a step forward and lifted his jaw at them. He wasn't daring them to do their worst, because they could, but he hadn't once backed down in his life. He wasn't about to start today.

Xiomber joined him a moment later, standing at

his side through thick and thin, like his egg-brother always had. They were a team, going back decades. Maybe Mom had never understood why they could never get real jobs, but she had loved them both anyway.

And nobody else had been good enough to do what Morty and his brother had accomplished. Y'all keep that in mind, too, suckers.

"Your soul has been read," *Speaker For The Communion* continued in a voice just as serious as Morty's was sarcastic. "Each glyph has been noted and filed."

Morty hadn't really grasped what true power was until he realized that those people could create a perfect copy of him tomorrow if they wanted to, just from the amount of information they had stored, like organic computers with a nearly-infinite drive array.

Morty refused to show fear. They knew it was there, but they knew everything.

"Your punishment should be the greatest," Speaker For The Communion said. "But others have spoken in your defense."

Morty felt a presence walk up behind him, like someone had just put up a skyscraper and suddenly he was standing in its shadow.

Gareth put a hand on his shoulder in companionship. Xiomber, too.

"Kid, we've known this was coming from day one," Morty turned to look up at the Star Dragon who had shaped so much of their lives.

"I don't care," Gareth stated flatly. "Evil never recognizes itself as doing wrong, so it never reconsiders its actions. It certainly never tries to step back and fix things. Sure, both of you have decades of other things to account for, but I've already heard that list, including all the parking tickets, jaywalking, and library fines. You still decided that you had to save the *Accord of Souls* and sacrificed almost as much as I did in the process."

Morty wasn't going to cry. Not even Gareth could make him, but it was a close thing. Xiomber and several others all seemed to have colds coming on, though.

So maybe a human could qualify as an egg-brother, too.

Grodray surprised the absolute hell out of Morty by stepping up on the other side and adding a hand on the other shoulder.

"You tried, Morty," that big, dumb cop said in a soft voice.

Damn it, I was doing fine holding it all together, Grodray. Why can't you just let me be killed in peace? It's unseemly to be crying while the gods snuff you out.

"As I said, others have spoken for you and your egg-brother," *Speaker For The Communion* announced in a softer tone. "Half of your actions warrant your execution as a warning to all future generations. But the other half cast you into a new light, one that we will hope foreshadows your ability to be properly rehabilitated by the Constabulary. Prime Investigator Jackeith Grodray already intends to ask the Court for a sentence of ten years to life, contingent on good behavior. We find that sufficient for you and your egg-brother. Perhaps you will meditate further on the nature of sin and redemption, and be able to make something useful of your future existence."

Morty thought he might collapse. But for the hands of the two Vanir cops on his shoulders, somehow giving him strength, he might have. He couldn't stop crying, but that was okay. Vanir cops had spoken up for him. It didn't get any weirder than that.

But if you burn the house down, you got no call to bitch about having to sleep in the mud. He and Xiomber had managed to call the fire department in time to save the *Accord of Souls*. Ten years in a small box would be just enough time to read everything in the prison library, and then get bored enough to start writing his autobiography. Somebody needed to tell these people *WHAT REALLY HAPPENED!*

Might as well be the truth.

FRIEND

TALYARKINASH CONTAINED as many of the tears as she could, which wasn't that many, all things considered. Morty and his brother had utterly upended her life twice. First by bringing her Marc Sarzynski to upgrade, and everything else that might have gone with it, perhaps.

Second, Gareth.

How could one word contain everything? Even the glyphs of The Communion were barely sufficient in their data-density to sum up what had happened since a human cop had walked into her lab and proposed to save the *Accord of Souls* with her help.

"Talyarkinash Liamssen," *Speaker For The Communion* turned the spotlight of his attention on her next.

She stepped forward, surprised when Pippa and Fatima came with her, adjusting wordlessly so that she was suddenly at the apex of their triangle. Two women she had met less than an hour ago, and they stood with her like Gareth and Grodray had done with Morty and Xiomber.

She squeezed their hands in thanks.

"Your crimes rank perhaps one step less than the two Yuudixtl," the Chaa continued. "But you worked in ignorance when modifying Marc Sarzynski, and with intent when presented with Gareth Dankworth. Like Morty and Xiomber, your actions show a growth and maturation that we find mitigates your sentence."

Talyarkinash nodded. That about summed it up: a decade of pure greed and subtle evil, and then everything since that moment dedicated to saving the *Accord of Souls* from her own actions.

"As with the Yuudixtl, the Constabulary will see to your punishment," the being announced. "We find in you the opportunity for true rehabilitation, and not just the punishment of social isolation. We also note your intent to continue working with the others to improve the galaxy, rather than simply working with a Damoclean Sword overhead. The Constabulary could free you tomorrow and your essential beliefs would no longer bend towards evil."

It was a good thing that Nari didn't blush like the furless species did. Gareth probably knew her well enough to see the whiskers twitch, and the ears rotate, but hopefully the rest would be ignorant.

This was what growing up felt like. Taking responsibility for helping others, and not just yourself.

For building a longer table, rather than a higher fence.

Pippa and Fatima both stepped close and engulfed her in a hug that said more than anything words might possibly contain. A moment later, she felt Gareth wrap his arms around the entire group and then his love for them all flowed, even Fatima, who had been a complete stranger.

But that was Gareth.

It was Eveth Baker grasping her after the others stepped back that broke something inside her, and she could no longer contain the tears. But the tall woman just held her close, like her mother had once done.

Around them, she felt even the *Ascended Chaa* smile down at her, once she finally could stand on her own, although Baker kept an arm around her shoulders like a sister. And Pippa stayed on the other side, with Fatima close enough to catch her if she fell backwards.

"Now we must confront true evil," *Speaker For The Communion* announced in an angrier voice.

Talyarkinash felt a polite force brush her to one side, clearing a pathway into which Marc's various sidekicks and hangers on were thrust.

Two Warreth women: Maiair and Yooyar. Both young, perhaps just barely adults as the *Accord* might measure things, but already hardened criminals and killers.

Two Nari men: Zorge and Mishalska. One old and one barely older than the Warreth sisters.

Seven humans. Two-Gun Kowalski. The crimeboss O'Rourke and his gang: a young woman whose purpose was obvious and four other gunmen who almost looked like the two-dimensional caricatures of humans everyone seemed to have in their heads.

Talyarkinash wondered if she was too used to the

five powerful beings around her as representatives of the species, and the others would truly be what humans were like, when viewed on this plane of existence. She would have to ask Royston, if she had the chance, or perhaps one of the survivors.

"The human associates of Bigby O'Rourke are mere criminals, caught up unknowingly in the greater tides of history," *Speaker For The Communion* intoned. "Human law can deal with all of you, but we will add one geas to your punishment. Upon incarceration, each of you will be compelled to detail all of your crimes for the authorities, that you will serve sufficient time in prison to have the opportunity to learn regret and be rehabilitated. The examples of Talyarkinash, Xiomber, and most importantly Morty should serve you as examples."

In the blink of an eye, six of the humans were gone. Somehow, Talyarkinash was certain that they had all just been dropped into a prison cell, somewhere on Earth, with the glyph of a Chaa welling up inside them for enough notebooks to contain their multitude of sins.

Minor players, serving only as examples of what the Chaa might do, even on a day that they had found the capacity for mercy. Especially the one known as *Merciless*.

"Two-Gun Kowalski, your glyph is known," *Speaker For The Communion*'s voice suddenly was filled with an anger she had not detected earlier. "You are a flawed example, even for the psychotic and homicidal humans. You lack the possibility of empathy that might someday lead to remorse. Time spent in prison would be dedicated to pretending to be rehabilitated that you might fool a warden into releasing you."

Talyarkinash watched the weak glyph of Two-Gun Kowalski snap his fingers at the gods around him.

"We find no redeeming qualities about you, human," *Merciless* spoke up. "Even as others of your kind have impressed this conclave with their wit, intelligence, and empathy. You are a waste of resources and will be dealt with as such."

This time, a flash of light seemed to descend on the human and engulf him. Rather than blinking out of existence, as the others had, he seemed to dissolve over the space of a second, like sugar dropped into hot water and stirred.

Probably a better death than he deserved, all things considered. She had seen what kind of person Kowalski was. Even at his worst, Marc Sarzynski still retained a core of humanity, of empathy, that she had been able to detect today. Two-Gun Kowalski had been a broken man, a rabid dog to be put down because there was nothing else one could do with him.

At least it was silent, both physically and emotionally.

"And now, broken children of the *Accord*, we come to you," *Speaker For The Communion* addressed the four remaining criminals. "We created this place for all species to live and grow in harmony by creating an accord that linked all into one being. You represent our failures, broken children."

The acid that he dripped on those words was heart-rending, as Talyarkinash listened. They saw themselves as parents who had failed to raise good children.

Worse, they would punish those children for it.

"Wait," Talyarkinash managed to bubble up a glyph from the depths of her own soul, interrupting the others.

As before, all eyes turned to her, most of them hostile now, as the Chaa worked themselves up to the sorts of anger necessary to punish their own children.

"Can you not fix them?" she asked.

"Fix them?" *Last Traveler* asked, after being silent for so long. "Why would we fix them?"

"Because they were born without accord," Talyarkinash felt the pleading in her tone but couldn't help it. "They lack the link to others that is the psionic resonance known as the *Accord of Souls*. Others do as well. After five Chitra, the bonds have grown weak."

Talyarkinash stepped closer to the four and breathed in the scent of their glyphs. Yes, criminals guilty of terrible things, but utterly bereft.

At least she had maintained some empathy, so she perhaps wasn't as broken as these others, but she had found her way back. They were to be destroyed without any opportunity to experience the love and friendship that most of the *Accord* took for granted.

But then, wasn't that true of most criminals?

"Only partly," another voice intruded on her thought processes.

Talyarkinash turned as she recognized the glyph from Pippa. Fatima joined her a moment later, sharing a memory of a conversation the two women had had previously.

"Most war and crime is a result of want," Pippa

had said then and Fatima glyphed it now, speaking of the human capacity for development, but unknowingly describing the underlying failures evident in the *Accord of Souls* as well. "Of poverty, both physical and emotional. As Roosevelt once said, freedom from want will lead up to freedom from fear. If we could move past poverty at a global and systemic scale, humans can be fantastically warm and giving people."

"The same can be said of the *Accord*," Fatima added, turning to encompass all of *The Communion* with her fierce gaze. "Crime today is a factor of want as much as it is of broken individuals choosing crime. Without need, they would have no reason to turn to the uglier side of life. The *Accord of Souls* is broken because too many people are not sufficiently engaged in productive lives, in the sorts of personal art that improve the species. All species and not just mine."

Talyarkinash turned and discovered that she had formed the gestalt again, three souls almost one, despite being Human, Nari, and Grace.

Or perhaps because of it.

Criminal (however reformed), outsider, cop.

"Yes," Pippa glyphed powerfully, drawing elements and knowledge from all three. "The Constabulary has been fighting a losing war for centuries to prevent crime. To contain it."

"Is this true?" *Narrator For History* suddenly reached out an angry hand and two other beings joined the trio at the center of the room.

Accord Commissioner Petim Diazal, representing the government. First Inspector Anen Wardson, of the Constabulary.

A tiny male, standing shoulder to shoulder with a

giant woman. Confronting the very gods themselves, returned angry.

The gestalt stepped up and stood beside them. Another one joined on the other side a moment later.

"It is," Wardson said simply. "The Vanir, as *Those Left Behind* have the greatest investment in the *Accord*, but that very commitment has alienated many others. Civilization has been breaking down for a long time, one bad choice at a time, in spite of everything my officers could do to hold it together. Thus the fear of humanity as too great of a stress for the system to survive."

"And all our efforts to bring more people into a greater understanding and support of the system have not been enough," Diazal added. "We have lost too many souls to alienation and lethargy. To crime and despair."

"So we are to take this foursome as an example of what has gone wrong with the *Accord of Souls*?" a new voice chimed in as the part of the entity known as Talyarkinash watched and listened. "And our own culpabilities?"

Uplifter, who had given the seventeen species form and capability. The other *Creator*, if you wanted to envision an entire pantheon of gods, all searching for the most powerful, but gods nonetheless.

"Five Chitra have passed," Talyarkinash spoke. Or perhaps Pippa. Or even Fatima. It was hard separating them into constituent parts at present. "None of you could see the future, so you could only establish a path, but not guarantee it. As with all, it is now necessary to correct the course against the drift of more than six hundred lifetimes lived."

"Fix all of the *Accord*?" Uplifter probed.

"Reinforce accord itself," they answered in harmony. "Strengthen the ties that bind. Let the lost children come in from the cold."

"Some will resist," Uplifter challenged.

"Resist a god?" the gestalt mocked the being. "Epicurus would laugh in your faces, were he able. *If a god is unable to prevent evil, then ze is not all-powerful. If ze is not willing to prevent evil, then ze is not good. If ze is both willing and able to prevent evil, then why does evil exist?*"

Talyarkinash had never heard of the Hellenic philosopher Epicurus before now, but was stunned at the jar of power that rocked the Chaa assembled here to *Judge.*

Rocked them to their very cores.

They recovered quickly, but the entire conclave had seen them learn doubt. Experience it firsthand for the first time in perhaps Chitra.

Perhaps they learned shame as well, if she read the glyphs correctly. That was the other side of a coin marked arrogance.

"You would need less Constabulary," someone up there challenged the First Inspector.

Nobody was prepared for the laugh that emerged from Wardson's mouth.

"I can think of no greater success than to spend more time rescuing people from emergencies and less time arresting them," she called back. "I would retire tomorrow and take up watercolor painting, if I thought that we would be needed less and less."

The *Ascended Chaa* vanished again.

Talyarkinash had no doubt that this vote would be just as contentious as the one to save humanity had been, but they had made a collective case to the Chaa.

As the running joke in the underworld had always gone: *How bad could it be if the Chaa didn't come back to stop you?*

Except they had. That was how bad it had gotten.

Talyarkinash could see new religious movements springing up, merely from the joy of having lived through such a thing as to watch all the gods return.

Abruptly, the gods returned.

Not there, and then present.

"Your jails will be overfull, when we act," *Narrator Of History* announced to the group. "Many more than you expect will return to the fold."

"So be it," the Arawath Commissioner replied. "We can always sentence them to the community service of helping their fellows rehabilitate. And I am sure that there are many murals to be painted, and parks that could be cleaned, by way of serving penitence. The *Accord of Souls* has never been about punishment. The goal was always to make the galaxy a better place to live, for as many beings as we could. It was only in falling short of that dream that we have failed. That you have failed, but only in your ability to envision far enough into the future to understand today's needs."

"It was never our goal to return again and again," *Narrator To History* replied. "We seek the *First Cause*."

"And yet, you are our elders," the small man said. "Our role models. If it is to be that we will face the *Creator* before you do, it is your duty to help prepare us, just as it is our duty to honor and reflect your values when you finally join us."

Talyarkinash found that last bit a trifle thick and

gooey, but she had never had any patience for the sort of glad-handing that was necessary if one wished to pursue political power as a vocation. Perhaps that was simply the nature of the game.

"So *The Communion* agrees, speaking for the *Ascended Chaa In Conclave*," *Speaker For The Communion* pronounced. "The *Accord of Souls* will be altered. All beings will feel our touch. Few will feel our wrath, but there are those that cannot be saved, even by such as us, and they will join the human in dissolution."

For a moment, the entire universe seemed to ring, like church bells calling the faithful. Talyarkinash felt something touch her deep inside, and then pass, like the kiss of a flower petal on a spring breeze.

"Now we will deal with the three humans who have caused us to return."

FALLEN

HE HAD KNOWN the moment was coming, but there was nothing Marc could do to prevent it. He had never gotten up one morning and decided to embrace evil. Never even thought of himself that way until recently.

Ambition was a relentless taskmaster.

At least there had been the chance to talk to Gareth. To acknowledge everything that had gone wrong, and assume the blame for it, as much as a younger version of Marc Sarzynski had deflected everything onto the other man before.

He was going to die, but he could do that with a clear conscience. He had done evil things in his anger. Later, because nothing less would keep the other gangs at bay, when this same man had been pursuing him across two different galaxies, first for Earth Force Sky Patrol, and later for the Constabulary.

Gareth wouldn't have stopped short of death, and based on the things Marc had learned today, he wasn't even truly sure now that death would be all that much of a barrier to Gareth's unstoppable rage. They had transcended into another place.

Marc felt the hands of one of the Chaa draw him front and center again, even as the remaining members of his gang vanished. But they were returning home, chastened by the power of these beings such that they would never again be criminals. The *Accord of Souls* would become so much stronger. Another would-be conqueror would utterly fail where Marc might have succeeded.

One tiny part of his soul held onto that tidbit, even as he had let the rest go. He could have succeeded, were Gareth not there to stop him.

But Marc Sarzynski had grown appalled at where his ambition would have taken him, once he had the chance to stop and truly consider that future, rather than spending every waking moment trying to stay one step ahead of the Constables.

Ahead of a Star Dragon.

Emperor Marc the First, if he had lived long enough to hand power down to one of his children. And the Chaa hadn't noticed him first and decided to undo things.

Yesterday, they had been merely the sorts of founding legends primitives told in order to justify themselves, and let their kings claim descent from gods.

Except there really were gods out there. And in here.

Marc drew a breath and let one true regret linger. He had chased Pippa, and that other Marc might have turned out acceptable, had she not broken his heart in ways he just never got over.

But there was another. She had broken his heart as well, although she would never know it. Her betrayal had been all the worse, for what it had engendered, but she was still perhaps the very model he would have used, when he went to Earth to select an Empress for himself.

As if she could hear his thoughts, Talyarkinash turned now and met his eyes.

Marc sighed at what might have been and turned to face his defeat.

"Marc Sarzynski, your list of crimes is so long that *The Communion* itself will adjudicate your punishment," *Speaker For The Communion* said simply.

Marc bowed his head and let go the breath he had been holding. Two-Gun Kowalski was most certainly in hell by now, and he would be joining the man shortly.

Drawing images from Gareth's mind, shared during the gestalt, the galaxy would truly be a better place without Marc Sarzynski in it. He shrugged. Not much more you can say about a man at that point.

"And that's where you're wrong, Marc," Gareth suddenly said aloud.

Marc's eyes flew open to find his oldest friend and deadliest enemy standing close.

"I know he had done evil, terrible things," Gareth said to the assembled vengeance above them. "But I also see the kernel of truth, or goodness at the core of the man. There is repentance for his deeds, little good though that he expects it will do him. I've just watched you alter an entire congress of species. Why can you not fix what ails Marc Sarzynski?"

Marc felt his jaw drop open. Gareth Dankworth

had been *Nemesis* for so long that it was sometimes hard to remember what came before. Both of them remembered the rage, that night when a Star Dragon was born.

And yet, they had transcended everything else.

Standing in the hall of the gods for final judgment did that.

"Why?" Marc turned to Gareth, almost forgetting those above in his shock. "I'm evil. You know that. Nothing would change what I've done. Nobody can bring those lives back."

"I know that, Marc," Gareth said. "But I also remember the man that many thought would one day lead Sky Patrol. Who would embody that thing we all strove for. Repentance means you regret what you've done. Rehabilitation means that you could still do good in the world. I believe you still have that good in you."

"Truly, Star Dragon?" *Mountain* called down. "You believe that he could be made a productive member of society without falling back on the old ways, the old evil?"

"I do," Gareth turned and challenged the very gods with his solidity.

"Would you be willing to trade your life for his, on that belief?" *Mountain* asked.

"Yes."

Marc nearly cried, much like the two Yuudixtl had. He had forgotten what it was like to have true friends. Perhaps he hadn't known one in the years since he and Gareth had parted ways.

"Marc Sarzynski?"

"No," Marc yelled back with all his might. "I will not allow it. You will not find a higher example of all the best of humanity that Gareth Dankworth. You should be holding him up for everyone to emulate, even knowing that in falling short they will elevate all things."

"Marc, all I ever wanted was for you to find peace," Gareth said. "To be happy. I've done the thing that would save everyone. You should have a chance."

"Don't you see, Gareth?" Marc implored him. "I can never undo those crimes. I can never make it right."

"That is where you are wrong, Marc Sarzynski," a new voice broke in.

Astray In Darkness. The darkest, bleakest of the gods.

"Wrong?" Marc almost demanded.

"We have both walked in shadows," the man said. "We have both gone *traik*. But it is possible to find one's way home. I am no longer *Astray In Darkness*, for I have found my path now. You should do the same. I will take the name *Polaris*, for the star by which Human navigators in the northern hemisphere of your world could sail their primitive ships and find their way home."

"The Star Dragon would speak for Marc Sarzynski," *Speaker For The Communion* called. "As would *Polaris*. Who would gainsay them?"

Silence, on a practical as well as psionic level, and Marc found he could sense those things now.

He felt a touch, almost a kiss on his cheek from a proud father. Everything seemed to settle in his soul and his eyes cleared from the tears.

He found Gareth standing shoulder to shoulder with him, like in the old days.

"If he is to return home healed, I would ask the *Ascended Chaa* a favor," Talyarkinash was suddenly standing close enough that he was able to reach out and take her hand.

The Communion paused.

"That can never be undone, Talyarkinash Liamssen," *Narrator For History* spoke. "The barrier will prevent it, and we will not be present to hear your regrets."

Marc felt something stir as she turned to study him. He had not forgotten her cobalt-blue eyes, or the Imperial Russian blues to her gray fur. Until her betrayal, he had considered other dreams.

Her eyes held a pleading question in them, one that took Marc's breath away.

"Are you sure?" he whispered to her.

She smiled at him, with eyes, whiskers, and ears.

"I am."

Marc hadn't realized that he could become more emotional than escaping a sure death, but he suddenly was. The gravity of her decision weighed on him like somehow walking on the surface of a neutron star.

"And I, as well," Marc offered weakly.

"Would any offer challenge?" *Speaker For The Communion* asked the room.

Marc waited on pins and needles, but nobody spoke.

"It is good," *Speaker For The Communion* announced. "*Uplifter*, I think it would be most appropriate in your hands."

Marc watched a blue light rise, like a whirlwind of cerulean sand, and Talyarkinash disappeared inside it.

A moment later, it evaporated, leaving behind a vision Marc found as compelling as *Venus Rising*.

It was still her, still Talyarkinash Liamssen, but she had been transformed. She was human now, rather than Nari, with those same eyes, but no whiskers, and human ears. The hair on her head was still the Imperial Russian blue it had been before, with gray and black stripes in it where it tumbled down to her shoulders.

Marc realized that she was nearly as tall as he was, but when he turned to his right, he realized that he was staring Gareth in the center of the man's chin.

His mouth fell open in awe.

"Correct, Marc Sarzynski," *Uplifter* smiled down at him. "Many chose to speak for you, so we will parole you to live out a human life on a human world."

He found Talyarkinash's hand, human now, and pulled her close to him. He even kissed her when her arms went around him and she insisted.

This woman would be giving up everything, choosing eternal exile on an alien world, and losing all her friends and family, but Marc also realized that she didn't really have friends or family, save for Gareth.

And she had chosen him.

Maybe he could be happy.

"That is settled," *Speaker For The Communion* glyphed. "Royston Loughty, we must consider your crimes next."

SEEKER

ROYSTON CONSIDERED the beings around him. The many things he had learned today, forming a new entity in the gestalt with Marc and Gareth. Discovering the other gestalt with Pippa, Talyarkinash, and Fatima.

He would never think of her as other than Fatima, in spite of it merely being a role that a Grace woman named Ilak Vorta was playing. He had never met that stranger, only the one purporting to be the niece of his old friend Firuz.

But Humanity was protected. As was the *Accord of Souls*, in some esoteric way that would see it almost reborn into a newer, stronger entity. And many criminals had gotten their just desserts.

"The wars of Maximus and the Star Dragon created a desperate situation, Royston Loughty," *Speaker For The Communion* intoned severely, his entire being seeming focused on Royston. "However, it was your effort to open the portal that represented the greatest threat to the galaxy in seven Chitra, as humanity would have found the path to reach nearby stars in perhaps as little as a century. Less, had their fears played upon them, to know that aliens truly existed out there."

Royston nodded. Truly, he had done the most, having taking the starting point of Gareth's kidnapping and relentlessly pursuing his investigations, until they led him to a bunker in the Arizona desert, and a special, lucky catseye that he had traded two silverfish and a bloodstone to Tommy Wilson for.

And a hole in the universe itself.

There were many steps on that path, but he had taken them.

"We have undertaken to understand a new humanity today," *Speaker For The Communion* continued. "Seven Chitra removed from your primitive forebears. Five of its most powerful representatives stand before us."

Royston considered his compatriots. Gareth and Marc collectively represented the very best that Earth Force Sky Patrol had ever striven for. He himself was the foremost expert on solar radiations in the entire Solar System, and a close competitor to Sir West, still hiding somewhere around here watching, when it came to raw physics.

Pippa was perhaps the most intelligent, most capable woman he knew, across a lifetime of powerful females. She even outscaled the members of the *Accord* that he found surrounding him now.

And Ellen Ames. How does one describe the Goddess of Music herself, descended to Earth and incarnated in such an avatar? Nothing Royston had attempted would have succeeded without the gestalt he had somehow been able to form with that woman and her band.

What were future humans going to be capable of, if this group represented the promise of that destiny?

"That is the question that has bedeviled *The Communion* time and again, Royston," *Docent*, the *Great Teacher* spoke up now, drawing their conversation into the personal, as if everyone else in the room were mere witnesses.

He studied the being, reading the glyphs of the man he had once been, one of the oldest and truest friends with *First Immortal*. This was the one who had showed the others of the *Ascended Chaa* how to translate themselves out of corporeal existence once she had done it, that they might grasp enough immortality to find the *Path of God Herself Written In The Stars*.

"Some have advocated for removing you and Ellen entirely from the context of Earth," he continued in a deep, broad voice that seemed to echo of the stars themselves. "They are driven by a fear that you might yet surpass us in depth and breadth of your power."

Royston tasted the magnitude necessary to achieve that sort of outcome, and felt it take his breath away.

How many Chitra would that take, even at the astounding pace that humans had developed since conquering fire?

"That, my friend, is why *The Conclave* will return in only half a Chitra," *Docent* smiled at him privately. "That will be sufficient time for Humanity to choose a direction, either towards power or evil, or perhaps they will have destroyed themselves before we return."

Yes, he supposed so. These gods might yet fear what humans could do, having seen the five beings of power of the current generation. It left Royston a little in awe, but he also understood why they had been able to achieve so much.

"How likely is such a concentration of power to occur again?" he asked the *Great Teacher*.

Amazingly, the Chaa shrugged back.

"We have studied the pattern of human genetics that each of you carry within," he replied. "Within the grand depths of ten billion humans, statistical analysis suggests it is low, but we also know that the five you will not be subsumed into the greater whole to disappear. Your various descendants will contain that spark, at the very minimum."

"You do not foresee a regression to the mean?" Royston asked.

Again, a simple shrug, as if the Chaa truly were incapable of such an extrapolation.

That might be where and how humanity could pass them, if we contained the seeds of the Oracle of Delphi.

"I have been alive for twenty-nine Chitra, Royston," *Docent* said, containing in his glyph a measure of what three hundred thousand human years might reveal. And what it might conceal. "All things are eventually possible."

All things are eventually possible?

Royston sighed and smiled, regretting, finally, that he would not be around to see them. He understood now what it meant that this group had chosen to live forever, rather than allow death to shortcut them to the *Creator Of All*. What might they miss here, if they passed on to another place and could never return?

That brought a feeling of brotherhood with this ancient being, this god descended to speak with a mere human. The Chaa who had become *Docent* had wanted to live long enough to see the everything that was possible.

Royston mourned that he would die first, but that was the nature of what it meant to be Human, and in that, he differed from the Chaa.

"Now, you see," *Great Teacher* nodded.

Suddenly, the rest of the room returned, as if that conversation had been truly private.

"I do," Royston nodded back.

They would leave him on *Earth*, where whatever mischief he might undertake would be small potatoes.

Even the first interstellar colony would not be a threat, because the clock had started, the walls were secure, and in five thousand years, this Judgment would continue.

"Royston Loughty, we note that your time is expected to be shorter than that of the others, as you have perhaps a few decades at most until death claims you," *Uplifter* spoke, drawing Royston's eyes away from *Great Teacher*.

"That is correct," Royston said quietly.

He turned far enough to finally spot Sir West, noting that the man had finally found his way into the center of the group, once there were no other places to hide.

"Members of *The Communion*, I would like to present my own mentor, Sir Westfield van Duren-

Abbott," Royston said. "He is perhaps as elderly as a human scientist can be expected to be, and retain that spark of life and intellect that makes him such a challenging foe."

And it was rather rude fun to watch a man like Sir West blush. But he deserved it, both the good and the bad.

"It is a pleasure to make your acquiaintance, Sir West," *Uplifter* replied politely. Others did the same with their glyphs.

"Royston, we have received a request."

Royston felt his chin come up. Not quite defiance, but he was no less adamantine in his outlook than either Gareth or Marc had been.

He was not prepared for Fatima to step close and study him from less than two feet away. Close enough to kiss her again, were either of them of a mind. And had the galaxy allowed it.

But the galaxy did. And the future would be upon them all too soon.

So he kissed her, reveling in the feel of all those tentacles tasting his hair and flesh as he did so. In doing so, he was able to read her soul, perhaps an after-effect of the gestalt he had contained.

Her vision nearly knocked him for a loop, so much so that he recoiled enough to look her in the eyes.

"You are audacity itself, my dear," Royston whispered.

She smiled demurely, looking very much the young Persian woman she was impersonating.

"My options as a deep cover agent seem to have evaporated, Royston," she said. "I have been *blown*, to use your term for it. Burned."

"And this would bring you joy?" he asked, contemplating how he might explain such a thing to his friends and family.

Except that Pippa stepped close and put an arm around each of them. So he knew what her vote was. Gareth joined a second later. Others did as well, reaching out to simply touch him on a shoulder or arm.

He had never experienced such a vote of confidence. But these were his friends and family. Even Alvin Siddall smiled at him and shook both their hands.

"Such will your destinies become intertwined with ours," Royston finally found *Uplifter* and smiled a knowing secret at the being.

"That is our hope, as well, Royston," *Uplifter* said. "Prepare yourself."

How does one prepare?

He took Fatima's hand in his and let his normally-tightly-held emotions flow into and over the woman, even as she did the same.

The blue flame descended, but it brought no pain.

When it cleared, he had to look at his hands, noting that the liver spots he had come to live with were gone. The color was better, as was the muscle tone.

So they had done it. He was thirty years old again, and Pippa could pass herself off as a younger sister, rather than a daughter.

And Fatima...

Her hair was black and long, lustrously flowing past her shoulders. The subtle, unconscious clues that might have suggested this woman was an alien were gone, noticed only because she was fully human now, and not merely pretending to be one.

She kissed him again, with promise. Decades of promise. Perhaps a second family, once he managed to explain everything to the bureaucrats who would not take the word of a mere god as evidence necessary to fill out new forms.

But that was tomorrow's problem. He had a honeymoon to consider first.

"Star Dragon, yours is the final decision."

STAR DRAGON

AND JUST LIKE THAT, they had come to the point that Gareth had been dreading all day. And perhaps for months.

What would become of him?

Ever since that moment when he had been standing in Talyarkinash's lab and she told him he would never be allowed to return to *Earth*. That no human could be allowed to know about the *Accord of Souls*.

They all knew now. He suspected it would haunt Humanity almost as badly as the thought of Humans had terrorized the *Accord* for so long.

Still, it was his time. He would not quail before it. Pastor Jacob had taught him to understand his place in the grand scheme of things, and nothing these Chaa had said or done would cause him to question that today.

Gareth stepped up and found *Speaker For The Communion* at the center of the line of Chaa.

"What would you have?" he asked simply, knowing that it no longer mattered.

Nothing really mattered at this point.

Gareth St. John Dankworth had accomplished everything he had set out to when Morty and Xiomber had asked him to save the universe. Even the totality that could be contained in the oath a new Deputy Agent of Earth Force Sky Patrol took when they earned their badge.

"You have no fear," the being observed.

It didn't feel like a question, so Gareth just shrugged his shoulders. He already knew that. Or rather, what fear all creatures knew would never be allowed to interfere with Gareth doing his duty. Doing what was right.

"The *Conclave of the Ascended Chaa* has spent the longest time in their debate on the merits of the Star Dragon," the being in charge said to the entire galaxy. "Until the decision was made to alter the very *Accord* itself, many were of the opinion that the galaxy needed such a protector."

Gareth nodded. He had come to the same assessment. The Star Dragon was a powerful symbol, inspiring fear among the criminals, as he had always intended, while also offering inspiration to the common folk that they didn't have to live with the criminality that had preyed on them for so long.

Already, Grace art had begun to incorporate his icon as a symbol for the Constabulary itself. Where he wasn't seen as a Herald of The Chaa themselves, like tomorrow might bring.

Gareth was uncomfortable with some of the religious movements that seemed to have sprung up, venerating him as some sort of archangel. It wasn't right. He was just a man, a cop trying to do his best.

"Similarly, arguments were offered for altering Humanity in a manner similar to how the *Accord* will change," *Speaker For The Communion* continued. "Thus would a Star Dragon perhaps become unnecessary."

"It is unnecessary now," Gareth countered them all before they got up too much a head of steam to derail. "The purpose of the Star Dragon was to provide a tool that could stop Marc Sarzynski and his intended conquest of the galaxy. That is done."

"The purpose, perhaps," the Chaa replied. "But the powerful symbolism remains."

Indeed. How much of Human history contained such a powerful image?

Pendragon. St. George. Bilbo. Beowulf.

Gareth St. John Dankworth?

Frightening to even consider.

"All I want to do now is go home," Gareth glyphed at the beings, trying to compress all the rage, the sorrow, and the anguish that had been his since that day. "To see my family again. To get on with my life."

"To make the world a better place," *Speaker For The Communion* finished the thought for him.

"As long as I breathe," Gareth whispered the promise.

"Without the Star Dragon?" *Speaker For The Communion* asked.

"Happily," Gareth replied, feeling his chin come up just the slightest amount.

It was a tool he had undertaken, and nothing more. His identify, much as others might not believe, was not wrapped up in a twenty-nine-meters-long bronze dragon, flying overhead and breathing fire.

"It is part of your genetic makeup now," the Chaa continued.

"So is being a Vanir, if I am given to understand the amazing genius of Talyarkinash Liamssen," Gareth nearly growled the words back. "Such was it with Marc, and you undid that. Undo the dragon from my soul and let me go back to being me."

"And thus, the crux of the argument, which grew quite heated by our standards," *Speaker For The Communion* said. "*Polaris*, who was once known as *Astray In Darkness*, and before that *Bowsprit*, you led the discussion. Let the people of the galaxy know your mind."

Gareth turned to face the newest of the Chaa, if you measured them by their souls.

He had been *Astray In Darkness*. Now he had found a polestar against which he could finally navigate, and it had turned out to be Humanity, of all things.

Thus, in questing, perhaps we all find the thing we seek.

"Indeed, Gareth," *Polaris* nodded to him. "We do find the thing we seek, even though we often cannot articulate what it is until it lands in our grasp."

Gareth had stopped being surprised that they could read his mind. In this strange place that he had been summoned, all things seemed possible. Arguing with gods was the least weird part about it.

Polaris laughed heartily.

"Many were of the same opinion, Gareth," Polaris said. "That the purpose of the Star Dragon had been fulfilled. That he was an unnecessary complication in the future planning of where Humanity might evolve, at a moment when the Chaa were shown to be deficit in such vision."

Gareth nodded. Exactly.

"But others felt that Humanity needed such a symbol, as long as they remained *unreconstructed* by the Chaa," the man continued. "That perhaps the very concept of the Star Dragon transcended even Gareth Dankworth and became a Human need. Your own historical studies reflect the continuing inspiration of dragons."

Pendragon. St. George. Bilbo. Beowulf.

"We would return you to *Earth*," Polaris said. "To Earth Force Sky Patrol, in their quest to bring Humanity to the very paradoxical place of no longer needing them."

Gareth felt a spike of fierceness overtake him. The First Inspector had said it best. If you don't need us, then we have succeeded beyond our wildest dreams.

"Humanity might not get there in the time remaining," *Polaris* cautioned him, marking that day, fifty centuries thus, when this conversation would be renewed with whichever of his descendants might have it. However they had gotten there.

"And?" Gareth prompted the being, when he realized that even a Chaa might know doubt.

"We would send you home," Polaris said. "And send the Star Dragon with you. If you are willing to hear my logic."

Gareth nodded. These were the most powerful beings in the galaxy. Maybe in the universe, ancient and hopefully commensurately wise.

"Humanity will need a Star Dragon, even after your time," *Polaris* said. "But we would make such a thing recessive within the core soul of Humanity itself, rather than linking it to your line. The next Star Dragon after you might and might not be any son or daughter of Dankworth."

"Pendragon," Gareth understood.

"Pendragon," *Polaris* agreed. "Already, you contain the myths of such a man, rising at need to fight injustice again. So shall Humanity have a Star Dragon today, and thus, perhaps, more Star Dragons later, if the need becomes acute."

"But not my children?" Gareth asked, finally anxious.

For so long, ever returning to Pippa's arms had been too much to hope for. Now, it was within his grasp, but what would it be like for his descendants, to be Dankworths, scions of such a famous man?

But if any could reach for the power, then they wouldn't necessarily need him.

He had been a hero, when the situation needed one.

Now he could just be a man.

Polaris nodded to him, and a blue fire erupted.

SKY MARSHAL

IT HELPED that every man he might have to deal with already knew the story. And the judgment of a panel of what might be gods.

Alvin Siddall was going to have one whale of an argument on his hands when he got home. And he didn't care. He was the Sector Marshal in charge of *The Arsenal*. Royston and Gareth, and even Pippa, fell under his jurisdiction. Marc Sarzynski would as well.

He remembered what the man had been like. Before.

The light in Sarzynski's eyes had returned. There was no other way to describe it. The same was in Gareth's eyes, now human again.

He turned to Royston and managed not to goggle at the man, suddenly three decades younger, or the woman that Fatima Darzi had turned into, holding his hand.

"Are you satisfied, Royston?" Alvin asked, with as much professionalism as he could manage.

"I am, my friend," the great physicist replied with a nod.

Alvin turned slowly in place, counting noses to make sure he had everyone.

Gareth and Pippa.

Marc and the now-human Talyarkinash.

Royston and Fatima.

Ellen Ames and her band: Tommy, Dave, Mick, Rhys, and Dalton.

Sir Westfield van Duren-Abbott, representing England, one of the Founders of Earth Force.

Across the way, a group of alien beings that would recede into legend shortly.

Yuudixtl.

Nari.

Grace.

Warreth.

Arawath.

Vanir.

Chaa.

Alvin bowed formally to the woman he recognized as his true peer: First Inspector Anen Wardson of the *Accord of Souls* Constabulary. She would actually be the equivalent of the Sky Marshal himself, Alvin's boss, but the rest of these folks were cops, like Gareth, or politicians.

Plus the hosts of Heaven and Hell, arrayed around him.

"I will speak for the *Accord of Souls*, when we must face the Sky Marshal and the governing bodies of Earth," Alvin nodded to the Chaa as well.

"And you will do us proud, Alvin Siddall," *Speaker For The Communion* replied with a bright tone to his voice.

One of the Yuudixtl separated from the rest of the crowd and stepped close now, drawing himself up proudly before Gareth before turning to smile at the rest of the humans.

"You did it, kid," Morty said to his partner in crime.

"We did it," the now-human Gareth agreed. "I couldn't have done it without you."

Both appeared to be in tears as they embraced, Gareth dropping to one knee and squeezing the tiny lizardman tight against his chest.

Alvin nodded, only tangentially embarrassed at such a display of emotion between two men, but it felt right.

Earth Force and Sky Patrol had taken a wrong turn. It was obvious now. Looking around at the many strong, capable women of the *Accord*, Alvin understood that things would need to change, going forward.

He could dedicate his remaining years to doing something about that. He had no doubt that the three women returning home with him would be powerful totems on his side.

Finally, the two separated. Gareth rose, and Marc Sarzynski stepped up and hugged Gareth as well.

Alvin heard Marc whisper something into Gareth's ear, but he was too far away to understand it.

He didn't need to. Those two had come home.

Now it was time for the rest.

Alvin looked up at the being who had apparently transformed itself during the course of this single day, taking a Human name to remember Human things.

He nodded to *Polaris*, glancing once to make sure that the two groups had separated, but he trusted these beings to be able to handle something so simple.

Polaris nodded back, smiling at him with pride. At all of them.

Light.

READ MORE!

Be sure to read all of the Star Dragon books!

Birth of the Star Dragon
Flight of the Star Dragon
Call of the Star Dragon
Shadow of the Star Dragon
Trial of the Star Dragon

ABOUT THE AUTHOR

Blaze Ward writes science fiction in the Alexandria Station universe (Jessica Keller, The Science Officer, The Story Road, etc.) as well as several other science fiction universes, such as Star Dragon, the Collective, and more. He also writes odd bits of high fantasy with swords and orcs. In addition, he is the Editor and Publisher of *Boundary Shock Quarterly Magazine*. You can find out more at his website www.blazeward.com, as well as Facebook, Goodreads, and other places.

Blaze's works are available as ebooks, paper, and audio, and can be found at a variety of online vendors (Kobo, Amazon, and others). His newsletter comes out quarterly, and you can also follow his blog on his website. He really enjoys interacting with fans, and looks forward to any and all questions—even ones about his books!

Never miss a release!
If you'd like to be notified of new releases, sign up for my newsletter.

I will never spam you or use your email for nefarious purposes. You can also unsubscribe at any time.

http://www.blazeward.com/newsletter/

Connect with Blaze!

Web: www.blazeward.com
Boundary Shock Quarterly (BSQ):
https://www.boundaryshockquarterly.com/

facebook.com/KRPBlaze

goodreads.com/Blaze_Ward

ABOUT KNOTTED ROAD PRESS

Knotted Road Press fiction specializes in dynamic writing set in mysterious, exotic locations.

Knotted Road Press non-fiction publishes autobiographies, business books, cookbooks, and how-to books with unique voices.

Knotted Road Press creates DRM-free ebooks as well as high-quality print books for readers around the world.

With authors in a variety of genres including literary, poetry, mystery, fantasy, and science fiction, Knotted Road Press has something for everyone.

Knotted Road Press
www.KnottedRoadPress.com

www.ingramcontent.com/pod-product-compliance
Lightning Source LLC
Chambersburg PA
CBHW070650100726

47907CB00007B/2161